THE OLD, OLD STORY, AND OTHER STORIES

A Collection of Science Fiction, Horror, Fantasy and Historical Crime Stories

by Andrew Lane

Published by Slow Decay Books

Collection Copyright © 2017 Andrew Lane

Second edition

A limited, signed and numbered first edition
of this book was published in 2017

Cover Art by John Swogger

ISBN: 978—1—9997945—4—5

Printed in Palatino Linotype font

Dedicated to Helen – my life for as long
as I have been writing these stories and
my wife for most of them…

CONTENTS

INTRODUCTION

I've loved reading short stories ever since I was a kid. I remember haunting my local libraries (yes, libraries in the plural – there were two within walking distance of my house, and I used to borrow books from both of them, sometimes on the same day) and taking out big anthologies with titles like *The Hugo Winners* (the Hugo being science fiction's biggest award) and *Alfred Hitchcock Presents: Stories to be Read With the Lights On*.

It seemed to me then, and it still does now, that there is something pure about the short story. Novels can wander all over the place before getting to the point, but with a short story every word counts, and you're trying to juggle not only plot and characterisation but also a *reason* for the story to exist. A novel exists to tell a story, but a short story (paradoxically) exists to make some kind of point about the world, or about human behaviour. At least, that's my opinion. Look, it's my anthology and I can have an opinion if I want. My gaff: my rules.

I'm reminded here, by the way, of a quotation originally attributed to mathematician Blaise Pascal and concerning a letter he had written. It has since re-attributed to various other people in various forms. "I have made this longer than usual because I have not had time to make it shorter." How very true of fiction as well as letters.

In the years between 1993 and 2007, while I was trying to build up a body of work as a novelist and journalist working in the field of TV and film, I would look for anthologies that had a window for accepting submissions and I would try to come up with a suitable idea I could send to the editors. I was also a member of a writers' group where we used to get together once a month and criticise each other's' work, and it was much easier to submit a short story than yet more chapters of an ongoing novel. Out of interest, other members of the writers' group included Charles Stross (now famous as a science fiction / horror novelist) and Ben Jeapes (who has written much admirable stuff under his own name and also under various pseudonyms for the Young Adult market).

There are, sadly, some stories I haven't been able to include in this collection. Primarily these are the ones where there is some kind of copyright restriction – stories set in the fictional universes of *Doctor Who, Blake's 7, Torchwood,* or Marvel's *X-Men.* Licensing being licensing, I couldn't see a way of being able to include them without paying strategically large sums of money to the licence-holders. Ah well – they're out there somewhere if you really want to look for them. EBay is a wonderful thing.

More recently I've written several stories using the character of Sherlock Holmes as invented by Arthur Conan Doyle, and several more set in the universe of H.P.Lovecraft's *Cthulhu Mythos.* I intend collecting these stories together in due time in two separate anthologies, which will be called *The Bizarre Investigations of Sherlock Holmes* and *Islands of Ignorance* respectively. Watch out for them. They, like this anthology, will be issued by my own little publishing company *Slow Decay Books*. There's a prize for the first person to email me with the reason why my publishing company has that name.

Oh, and one last note – these stories were originally published by a mix of English and American publishers and magazines. I have recovered the text for some of them from my computer files, but others I had to scan into my computer. In those cases I've retained the spelling chosen by the publisher / magazine, which means you will see some American spellings in the following pages. Don't worry about them.

Thank you for reading this. I hope you enjoy what follows. Please make sure you turn the lights off when you leave…

Andrew Lane
Dorset
November 2017

SAVING FACE

One of the cameras died just as Martle entered the studio.

It was lying on its back as he passed, its legs twitching as the last few sparks of life shunted randomly through its brain. He didn't even bother looking at it as he walked by. As far as he was concerned they always looked like dead meat, what with their unresponsive gazes and their slumped posture. Going tits-up was nothing unusual: something to do with the genetic trade-offs between brain development and lifespan, or so the brochure said. Some of the production staff were attempting a lacklustre revival, air-blasting drugs through its baggy hide and checking brain activity on a handheld monitor, but Martle could tell it wasn't any use. He'd already seen the vast bulk of the brood-mother up in the gallery shudder with pain, then shrug and look away from the body. The two other cameras huddled on the far side of the studio kept looking up at her for reassurance. Her lidless eyes slid over them without appearing to register their presence, but gradually they moved apart and stared vacantly at whichever wall they happened to end up facing.

"What's the prob'?" Martle said as he passed Welter. The camera supervisor shook her head.

"Fuckin' things," she muttered. "No fuckin' use.

No fuckin' use at all. I told them, last year I told them. 'Don't tell me about cleaner fuckin' edits and better-quality pictures,' I said. "If you haven't got the balls to uprate the cameras, they'll up and die on you. And was I wrong?" She headed toward the group of production staff, gesturing them irritably away from the body. "Only thing that one's good for now is fuckin' cat food" she said.

"Or public service broadcasting," said one of the group. The rest laughed and began to manoeuvre the body out of the studio.

Suzy Bowles was already at the long desk when he arrived, flicking through the pages of her script and checking her lead-in lines. Martle detoured round the autocue box and waved. Without glancing up, she flicked a hand in acknowledgement. As usual, in the ten minutes since the final script conference she'd acquired a visible layer of foundation, blusher, eye shadow and mascara. Normally she disdained ornamentation of any sort, and endured the daily makeup ritual with barely concealed contempt.

Martle rather liked it. He'd always enjoyed dressing up. "Five minutes, kiddies," shouted Greg, the floor manager, holding his earphones on with one hand and waving his clipboard toward the gallery with the other. "And we're making do on two cameras."

As Martle sat down and shuffled through his script he could hear Greg holding a discussion with the distant director. Eventually the orders were relayed.

"Change of plan," Greg yelled. "We're leading with Luxembourg." Lights flickered on the autocue as it was reprogrammed from the gallery. Martle and Suzy both unhurriedly reordered their pages. Bill Paternoster's script lay unopened in front of his empty chair.

"Two minutes," said Greg. "Where the hell's Paternoster?" Martle and Suzy Bowles both looked up and shrugged. Welter just looked blank and began to herd her cameras toward the news desk.

Heralded by a distant bellowing, Bill Paternoster came charging into the studio. Sweat beaded across his plump, flushed face. One of the makeup girls chased after him clutching a powder puff. He fell heavily into his seat beside Suzy Bowles and grinned disarmingly up at the gallery.

"Sorry," he shouted, "got held up over dinner."

"Had to finish the bottle, you mean," murmured Suzy, not really caring whether Paternoster heard.

"One minute," said Greg. "Quiet in studio, please. Stand by video. Stand by sound."

The bright studio lights intensified the musky odour of the cameras. Martle felt his heart speed up and the cool sheen of sweat spread down his back and across his chest. Twenty years, and still he felt it. Every night. He took a deep but quiet breath and forced his hands to unclench. His fingers left moist smears as he trailed them across the angled screen of the TV monitor set into the desk. He took a sip of water from the glass before him.

"Ready?" Suzy asked quietly. "Ready," he murmured. Greg's voice was loud in the sudden hush. "Thirty seconds." The autocue projected Martle's opening lines into the air before him, invisible to the eyes of cameras.

He let his gaze wander round the cramped studio, barely large enough to contain the news desk podium, the autocue, and the cameras. Skeletal lighting gantries filled the space where the ceiling should have been, and through the long, smoked glass window of the gallery he could see the production team, and the smooth, bloated outline of the brood-mother.

"Bob, to camera, please," said Greg. Martle's eyes met the single large pupil of the camera facing him: a deep black well without the slightest flicker of interest.

The red transmission light above the studio door blazed on. Greg swept his arm down. Martle's lips curved into a sincere smile.

"Fresh controversy as Brazil is accused of supplying arms to both sides in the Luxembourg riots," he said firmly. "A full report tonight in ECBS News."

Greg's lips mouthed the words "Go theme. Go titles." The ECBS logo rotated out of nothing on the monitor, changed colour, broke into pieces and reassembled into the words "ECBS NEWS-With Bob Martle and Suzy Bowles." A strident but unhummable tune with a strong backbeat faded up and then down.

On the monitor screen Martle's face appeared: filtered through the eyes of the camera, transmitted telepathically to the mind of the brood-mother, and taken by wires and by circuits from her brain to the mixing desk of the gallery. And from there to the world. -

"Good evening. This is the eight o'clock news from ECBS, brought to you by Tulley Alvarez Benita PLC. The headlines tonight: Forty killed today as fresh rioting breaks out in Luxembourg. We'll be talking to the man who says he's sold guns and missiles to both the mercenary forces and the Zen militants. Also: As the time approaches for the second batch of trade goods to be released by the Cimliss, we ask, 'Are we getting our money's worth?' As the go-slow amongst officers in the United States Air Force enters its third week, we talk to the Senator who says it should never have been privatised. And body-bepple: harmless fad or addictive habit? A special report."

"Smile," said the autocue. Martle's camera slumped as Suzy began to recite details of the headline story. Martle relaxed, took another sip of water, and watched the monitor admiringly as Suzy recited her lines with just the right mixture of professionalism and anticipation. Beneath the desk, out of the camera's line of sight, her foot beat out a nervous tattoo.

Following the pre-recorded interview which wrapped Suzy's story, Martle took over for the Cimliss piece. He'd calmed down since the first item, and this time managed to catch glimpses of the monitor out of the corner of his eye as he talked. It always amazed him how great the gulf was between appearance and reality. He could feel the warm trickle of sweat down his sides, but as far as the camera was concerned he was as casual and as authoritative as it was possible to be. During a preshot insert his image remained on the monitor, and he studied the three-dimensional display critically. His temples were greying, but his eyes were as clear as ever. No sign of a gut yet, despite the amount of junk food he lived on. And judging by the regular stream of proposals and invitations that were fielded by his secretary, the audience loved him as much as the camera did.

A monitor across the studio was showing the pre-filmed report, and Martle glanced over at it when Greg signalled the imminent change-over. Judging by what he could see, Julia Wood, the director, had taken the cheap and easy option: plenty of *vox pops* of local traders who wanted trade sanctions applied to Cimliss goods, with cutaway shots of ECBS cameras moving around the studio. The cameras were only one of the many items of biologically engineered trade goods that the Cimliss had offered to humanity, of course, but they were by far the easiest for ECBS to tape. The hospital companies were still wary of showing the medical instruments in case they scared away paying customers, and the Government weren't letting anybody near the weapons.

No shots of the Cimliss, of course, but their publicity-shyness was well known. The only footage of them in existence lasted five seconds, was owned by Eurostar and came with a price tag of a million dollars a second for any other station's use.

Oddly enough, Martle thought, the tone of the insert was considerably more innocuous than the earlier script conference had indicated it would be. It contrasted sharply with his own script, which suggested that the Cimliss had somehow palmed humanity off with shoddy goods. Even the local barrow boys seemed half-hearted in their condemnation of the Cimliss, and one or two were openly supportive. Bad direction, Martle thought. The insert made his piece look like hysterical conservatism. He would have to have a word with Julia.

The insert finished, and Martle handed back to Suzy. His camera pulled away to focus on Paternoster as Suzy ran through a brief résumé of the ongoing USAF work-to-rule. As she handed over to Bill for an in-depth political analysis of the latest events, her camera lumbered round on three clumsy legs to focus on Martle.

Paternoster had regained his breath by then, and the attentions of makeup had erased the sweat and covered the network of broken capillaries in his cheeks and nose. They couldn't do anything for his red-rimmed eyes, however, or for the haze of stale alcohol that perpetually hung round him and gave away his major preoccupation since his wife died.

The last item was a pre-recorded report which

they'd been trying to slot in for weeks. A leading story on the sudden disappearance of a TV evangelist had been dropped that afternoon when he was found doped up to the eyeballs and dressed in latex in a police cell. Station-to-Station had bought off all the witnesses for an exclusive, so ECBS were using the body-bepple story to fill the slot. It gave them all a chance to relax for a few minutes before Martle had to summarise the headlines again, wrap up the broadcast, and hand over to the continuity announcer. As soon as the red lights were off and the director pronounced herself pleased, they all collected up the pages of script that they had scattered over the desk and prepared to leave. As they walked through to have their makeup removed, Welter was herding the cameras back to their pens and the food sprays.

It was Paternoster who proposed a few drinks in the subsidised staff bar. "To help us unwind," he said, but Martle guessed that whether he and Suzy went along or not, Paternoster would be unwinding for the rest of the night. As usual, Martle felt drained and shaky after the broadcast. He was on the verge of refusing, but he couldn't stand the thought of anyone having fun while he wasn't around.

"Sure," he said. "But I need to collect some stuff from the dressing rooms. I'll meet you down there."

The most direct route to the dressing rooms was up a level and through the canteen, but at that time of night it would be locked up tighter than the producer's ass. Instead he took the elevator down to the basement and cut along the curved studio access corridor. The studios themselves were dark—the nine o'clock news was the last live broadcast until breakfast TV opened—but the lower levels were kept open for carpenters and lightning engineers getting ready for the next day's quota of porno-soaps and game shows. The heavy cinnamon smell of the cameras filled the air, and Martle could pick out their distinctive front-and-back toe prints among the scuffed boot marks and high-heeled scratches in the dirt of the floor. He paused, thoughtful. The cameras weren't supposed to be allowed out of the studio unless on outside broadcast, in which case they were taken out the back way. Perhaps there was another Inside Your ECBS feature on the way. When all else fails, when imagination and money run out, make a programme about yourself.

He walked on. The corridor curved gently away from him, circling the building. Studio One: *Fathers and Sons*, ECBS's top-rated porno-soap. Studio Two: the new game show *In for a Penny, In for a Pounding*. Studio Three: the ever-popular *Whips in the Cupboard*. Studio Four: dark ever since a young sculptor called Prewster had blown the top of his head off during the arts show *I Know What I Like*, leaving as his legacy a placard in his lap which bore the legend "Dead Artist, by Adrian Prewster" and a show cancelled so fast that the resulting vacuum sucked three ECBS board members into sudden unemployment. Around the curve of the corridor Martle could see the entrance to the fire escape leading up to the dressing rooms. And here, Studio Five, where every day, Martle and...

Light spilled out around the edge of the studio doors. Martle stopped dead. Recording on the news had finished for the day. They weren't scheduled for a change of set for months. So who was in there? The studio was protected from stray noise by two sets of double doors, the outer ones windowless and not quite meeting in the middle, the inner ones with round inset windows and boasting a crumbling rubber strip covering the gap between them. The light was coming through the uneven space between the two outer doors like a thin strip of summer.

As he crept forward, the possibilities sorted themselves in his mind. Could be vandals, squatters, vagrants, muggers, bailiffs... Could be anyone. Once he'd identified the intruders, he'd go and alert security, then fade quietly into the background and head off to the pub. He wasn't paid to be a hero. If there was one thing experience had taught him, it was not to get involved. He pushed his way through the first set of doors and put his face up to one of the windows in the second.

And turned away, blinking rapidly.

A trick of the light, surely. Or had someone slipped something into his water while he hadn't been looking?

He put his eye back to the windows. Across the

far side of the brightly lit studio the metal-mesh door to the camera pens stood wide open. The cameras themselves were milling around the newscaster's desk, alternately moving forward, backwards and sideways. One of the cameras stood away from the rest, moving rapidly round the outside of the group. There must have been at least ten present: almost the entire ECBS complement. And then the cameras drew back slightly, and Martle could see between them to the newscasters' desk.

Three cameras had squeezed their ungainly bulks into the form-fitting chairs. They were sitting upright, staring blankly at their companions. One of them was nodding slightly. As Martle watched, it turned to the camera beside it, which met its gaze, turned to its front and began to rock its head forward and back. The first camera turned away and looked down at the monitor on the newscasters' desk.

The whole bizarre, lumbering ritual was carried out in absolute silence, apart from the shuffle of their feet and the quiet wheeze of their breathing.

Martle pushed the doors open and strode into the studio. It wasn't until he stepped across the length of masking tape six feet beyond the threshold of the door, legacy of some long-forgotten scene-shifter, that Martle realised what he'd done. There had been no conscious decision. He just couldn't walk away. He had to know what was going on.

Martle's eyes were drawn to his right where a

small TV monitor stood on a stand, the one used by Welter for diagnostic tests. It had been switched on, and the flickering image captured and held Martle's attention. The picture was obviously being relayed from one of the cameras, and showed the newscasters' desk in medium long shot. By luck, because surely it couldn't have been judgement, no other cameras were visible apart from the three sitting at the desk.

Except that they weren't cameras. On the screen, so tiny that the pseudo-3-D effect was just a barely perceptible rounding of edges and softening of shadows, Martle, Suzy Bowles and Bill Paternoster were sitting in their usual places, staring quiet and watchful at a point behind the camera.

Martle looked up. Three cameras sat behind the desk, surrounded by their fellows. Back on the screen, three newscasters. Human newscasters. And behind the real desk, three bulky, alien creatures. His eyes moved from the cameras sitting behind the desk to the lone creature who, unlike his fellows, was facing away from Martle and toward the trio. From there the image was transmitted, mind to mind, up to...

Martle's eyes flicked upward to the long, dark window of the director's gallery. Through the glass he could make out the silhouettes of the monitor banks, the backs of the production staff's chairs, and the still, bloated bulk of the brood-mother.

The shadows hid detail and shrouded her in mystery, but Martle could -have sworn that she was smiling.

Movement on the floor caught his eye. The cameras were standing up behind the desk and shuffling into a new position. He looked at the monitor to make sense of the tableau. The pictures he saw made him feel hot, breathless and faint.

On screen Suzy Bowles was bent over the news desk, an expression of ecstasy contorting her features, her skirt hitched up over her back. She was applying lipstick to her glossy, parted lips. Martle saw himself standing behind her, his trousers around his knees, thrusting deeply into her. Sweat beaded his face and stained the armpits of his jacket. Paternoster, or rather his image, was throwing up convulsively over Suzy and the desk. His shirt and trousers were caked with vomit.

Martle could feel the world turning grey and pulling away from him as the shock bit home. He pinched himself, hard, on the back of the hand. The studio snapped back into glorious Technicolor and sharp focus. He let out a small, incoherent protest.

As if on cue, the cameras all stopped moving and turned to face him. Their unreadable stares formed a wall of alien indifference. Their leathery flanks rose and fell in unison. A feeling of expectancy filled the studio, as palpable as the spiced smell of the cameras.

How did they know? How could they know? He'd never told Suzy how he felt about her: he only rarely admitted it to himself.

How could they know? Against the barrier of their eyes he retreated, lost and alone. The doors parted at the pressure of his back. As they closed in front of him, cutting off the invisible thread that joined his gaze to theirs, he felt like a puppet whose strings had been cut. He stumbled along the corridor, handbag forgotten, through the turnstiles and out into the rain. There he walked aimlessly through stinging squalls for what seemed like hours before flagging a taxi and heading for home.

He dreamed, of course. He dreamed of a naive young newscaster stammering over an unexpected newsflash. He dreamed of fuzzy 2-D pictures, speckled with static, transmitted live by satellite from Ecuador. He dreamed of vast blue skies, and of steamy rain forests, and of Cimliss spacecraft spiralling lazily downward from the heavens like giant orange leaves, no two the same shape, size or shade, now drifting together, now drifting apart, before coming to rest upon the lush forest floor. And opening their doors for trade.

He went in to work the next day believing that it was all a dream, but knowing that it wasn't. He watched carefully for signs from the cameras, but they stumbled about the studios giving nothing away. If they had anything to give.

During the script conference Suzy and Bill were sarcastic about his failure to make the bar, but an extemporised story about having to escape from a persistent female fan who had cornered him outside the door kept them sweet. Like the cameras, he stumbled un-thinkingly through the day.

The lunchtime broadcast was a disaster. Halfway through an item on the long-running Argentinean oc-cupancy of the Antarctic, he caught sight of himself in the desk monitor. His hair was awry and his left eye appeared to have acquired a slow tic. Distracted, he started referring to the Antarctican invasion of Argentina, realised his mistake and lost his place on the auto-cue. The pitiless eyes of the cameras magnified his mistake. A bead of sweat became a wash. A slight tremor of the hands became a visible palsy. Martle stumbled his way through the rest of the broadcast and rushed to the toilets as soon as the credits rolled, but all he could see in the mirror was the same cool, slightly ironic face that greeted him every morning.

Makeup took longer than normal for the mid-afternoon session. Martle suspected that the producer had ordered special attention for him, but whatever the assistants did, it worked brilliantly. There was no script conference— the broadcast was essentially the same as for the lunchtime transmission— and when he left the makeup chair and strode into the studio he looked and felt immaculate.

It didn't matter. As soon as he could after the broadcast started, he glanced down at the monitor.

And froze in mid-word. His face was puffy and blotched, his eyes bloodshot. His hands appeared to tremble on the desk. The reflection of the overhead studio lamps made his forehead glisten through sparse, grey hair. Large beads of sweat trickled down his nose.

When it became clear that he wasn't going to continue, the director signalled for Suzy to start the next story. The cameras repositioned themselves, and, as Martle's camera lumbered away, it winked at him, slowly and deliberately.

Greg, the floor manager, approached Martle after the broadcast. "Bob," he said, "I think Julia wants a word." Up in the darkened director's gallery Julia Wood waited for him. For a moment, as he entered, she looked to him like a red-haired skull placed on top of a fashionably tailored dummy. Then the shadows shifted, she moved, and he could see the pale skin pulled tight over the bones by stress and exhaustion. The angled surfaces of the control banks behind her were rippling with lights, and Martle was uncomfortably aware of the soft, bloated silhouette of the broodmother in the corner of the narrow room.

"What the fuck is wrong with you?" she snapped. "Girlfriend died or sommat?"

How could he tell her? "Sorry, Julia," he said. "I don't know what came over me. Tired, I guess. Been pushing it a bit."

"This is twice today, Bob. Don't let it happen tonight."

"Look..." he said, and paused. "I... I think it may have looked worse on the screen than it actually was. I didn't feel that bad, and..."

"It's what's on the screens that pay our dosh," said Julia, "not what you feel like. Seeing is believing, Bob, and if the paying public, bless them, see you throwing wobblies on their TV set then they're going to switch channels. So, what you feel like isn't important, *capishe*, lover?

"No probs," Martle murmured. He shouldn't have been surprised. It was on TV. It had to be true.

"Okay..." said Julia. He could tell that she didn't want to leave it there, but she knew that as ECBS's top-rated newsreader Martle was besieged by offers from other networks. He might be on the way down, but there were a lot of rungs on the way. "Script conference in ten minutes. There's a couple of new stories coming down the line. Pull your shit together."

She walked toward the door, weaving a bit. Rumours had it that she was hitting drink, drugs, or both. To Martle she just looked terminally tired.

He moved to follow her, but a slow heaving in the far corner of the gallery caught his attention. He walked closer as the brood-mother shifted position, moving round to face him. The thick cables which emerged from her skull seemed noble rather than unnatural, a headdress for some pagan deity. Black insulating tape wound around them and attached them to the enlarged and roughened pores into which they plunged. Martle knew that her skull was riddled with naturally occurring fissures, through which the cables passed on their way to her brain. Somewhere along the way, blood vessels and nerves intertwined with them. By the time they reached their goal, they weren't cables anymore.

"What do you want?" he whispered. "What do you want?" There was no answer, of course. The brood-mother merely gazed incuriously at him, pulsing slightly as she breathed. He moved over to the window, but her eyes didn't move to track him. She didn't care about him, didn't even know he existed. His image passed through her mind every day on its way to the waiting world, but she was incapable of understanding its implications, its meaning or its connection to the man standing before her. Martle knew that. He turned to leave, but as he did so, his gaze passed over the window showing the studio floor far beneath.

Three cameras stood there, staring up at him. He met their gaze, knowing somehow that he wasn't being watched by them but by the grotesque bulk which rested beside him, until Welter walked over with her cattle prod and herded them back to their pens.

And behind him as he left he could hear a breathy pulsing that might almost be taken for laughter.

The conference room was crowded by the time he got there, and he squeezed into a seat beside Suzy Bowles. Various journalists and production crew were smoking, sipping coffee and chatting. Bill Paternoster was, to nobody's surprise, absent.

Julia Wood was sitting next to Chris Isher, producer of ECBS News. Isher, an ambling, bearlike man, sized Martle up before waving a hand in greeting.

"Okay kiddies, let's make a start," he said. "We'll be continuing on with the Argentina story, of course, and picking up on the latest Luxembourg developments, but today's big news is the speech this morning by the Foreign Secretary. Who caught it?"

A scattering of hands went up around the table. Martle's wasn't one of them. He'd been aware that the speech was scheduled, the weekly handouts of events had made sure of that, but he relied on the script conferences to keep him up to speed on current affairs.

"Okay," Isher continued, glancing again at Martle, "the upshot of it is that the Government want to renegotiate the terms of the Cimliss trade agreement when they arrive next month. Nobody is happy about the stuff we got last time: it works, but nobody knows why. The Government will be putting forward a twelve-point document which guarantees better servicing and support, and a ten percent refund of the cost of the last batch amortised against the new one. How do we play it? Any ideas?"

"Last night's item was fairly straight," Suzy said, twirling her fingernails idly against the table top. "Do we need an angle on this one?"

"There's a lot of feeling out there against the Cimliss," said Julia Wood. Her eyes flickered from person to person, almost daring argument. "We'll be climbing on a popular bandwagon if we condemn the Cimliss for cheating us. Not in so many words, of course, but it could be a ratings winner."

Small noises of agreement came from the assembled journalists. Coffee cups were raised in anticipation of a few seconds' grace before the next item. Isher took a breath, ready to pronounce.

"Hang on," said Martle, surprising himself as much as anybody else. "How are Station-to-Station going to be slanting it? Or Fox? Or NASAtel?" He looked around. Isher was frowning. Wood just looked pissed off. Suzy, bless her, was smiling encouragingly. "Everyone's going to be pushing the idea that the Cimliss have sold us shoddy goods. No matter which channel people switch to, they'll get the same story. Apart from one." He smiled, but inside he trembled with the anticipation of what he was about to do.

"I think we should go the other way. Look at it from the Cimliss point of view. Try and get inside their heads. It's business, right, not a charity. We knew that from day one. So did the Government, but now they're trying to change the rules."

He could see by their faces that they weren't convinced, but at least they were listening. Lines of wet warmth traced their way slowly down his sides, but on the surface he was the consummate professional.

He addressed himself directly to Isher. "Look, people are only going to watch us if we provide something that nobody else does. And we can with this piece. We can break away from the herd and give the other side of the story."

Isher was wavering.

"Put it this way," Martle continued, trying to consolidate his gains. "If we take the anti-Cimliss line, then whatever way it turns out, everybody will be sharing the credit or the blame. No brickbats, no bouquets, no awards. If we go pro-Cimliss and we're right, then we come out smelling of roses. Award-winning stuff."

That was what clinched it. Isher made one of his famous "my own feeling is" decisions, and they went on to other matters. Martle only caught odd scraps. He was too busy picking over the enormity of his betrayal. Bob Martle, the man who sold the world. And for what? To save face.

Or had he misread the entire thing? Was it possible? Had he taken a few odd scraps and built out of them a story the scale of which appalled him and held him helpless?

He might never know. Nobody might know, not for generations, but if in some future century the Earth was some economic satellite state of the vast Cimliss trading empire, a minor branch in a galactic suburb, would anybody trace it back, point the finger and say yes, it was him, he was the man?

After the meeting broke, he headed for makeup to prepare for the evening news. As he sat in the chair and the layers of makeup were applied over his skin and over each other, he felt the truth slipping away, becoming buried, until ultimately it was just another layer, another commodity to be bought and sold, no different from other people's truths.

As he entered the studio, one of the cameras walked past. He tried to catch its eye, but there was no flicker of acknowledgement, no sign of the vast contempt that he knew, from that little Charade he'd stumbled across the previous night, that they must feel for him and for all humanity. Up in the gallery the brood-mother stared out into the tangled lighting gantries, yet Martle felt sure that she was aware of his scrutiny, and that she knew what he'd done for her. And for himself. Part of him wondered why they'd waited until now to act, but another part already knew the answer. They were already acting: twisting intonations, moods, backgrounds and the occasional word to suit their own agenda. In his mind's eye he suddenly saw a global village linked by television: billions of people whose only opinion was delivered daily in discrete sound-bites. And he saw how fragile a thing was a career in the camera's eye.

Suzy Bowles came up behind him.

"Are you going to be okay tonight?" she murmured. "You were looking really rocky this morning."

Martle smiled, but inside he felt small and scared.

"Don't believe everything you see on television," he said.

NO EXPERIENCE NECESSARY

Two o'clock, and Allard still hadn't finished cleaning the third transpod. If he could be bothered to refocus his eyes from dreams and memories he could see it through the smears on the control-room window, bathed in jets of steam, down on the hangar floor. This one had the usual heavy charring around the field generators: carbon deposits carbon deposits enamelled onto the hull of the ship by the hysteresis field and the heat of re-entry. Sometimes he wondered what the pilots thought they were up to when they brought the transpods back to Earth. Most of them were too concerned with looking good to worry about wear and tear. Flashy landings might impress the girls, but they were hell on the bodywork. They should try his job for a while; that would teach them.

The spaceport was ten kilometres from the city: far enough away to smooth people's fears, if not actually improve their safety should an accident happen. If God forbid, some cocky pilot tried one flashy landing too many and cracked his reactors open on the landing apron the effects would be felt all the way to the coast, but ten kilometres was an acceptable compromise between the illusion of safety and the reality of convenience. Out of sight, out of mind.

Stifling a yawn, Allard gazed out into the darkness of the hangar. The spotlights that pinned

Transpod Three to the cracked concrete floor illuminated only the barest hint of the girders that braced the walls and supported the roof. Some of the spotlights reflected back from polished sections of hull and fanned out into the darkness. Dimly they illuminated the other transpods which were lined up regimentally in the shadows. The multiple reflections made numbers indeterminate, but Allard didn't have to examine the manifests to know how many to clean. The only time there had been any number other than six was when one of them had suffered a multiple field failure taking off from Tycho Base three years before and crashed in balletic slow motion to the surface of the moon. Although he had adjusted quickly to the five transpod schedule, Allard had sometimes caught himself towards the end of a shift peering into the shadows looking for the sixth. The replacement had come through quickly enough - after all, they were losing business without it - but one of the pilots later told him that they still saw the ghost of the old transpod occasionally, coasting gently between Earth and Moon. But then, everyone knew about pilots and their strange sense of humour.

Allard leaned forward and tapped some fresh instructions into the keyboard. One of the multi-jointed arms which hung from the ceiling of the hangar altered its position slightly in response. Allard watched with satisfaction as the steam blasting from the nozzle at the end dislodged more singed deposits from the hull. He was good at his job, nobody could deny that. Not even the pilots, with their contemptuous smiles and their childish jokes. It wasn't easy, knowing how to angle the jets to alternately weaken the deposits from the top and then lift them from the side. It took practise. And skill.

It was difficult to tell through the steam, but Allard thought he could see the last sheds of carbon fly away into the darkness. He turned off the steam jets to make sure. Transpod Three sat pristine under the spotlights, glistening as if newly born. Another dance on the keyboard and the insect arms lifted from the transpod as it rolled away into shadow. Allard glanced at his wristwatch and frowned. Two ten, and there were still three more transpods to clean. If he didn't have them finished for first launch at sun-up the day foreman would eat him for breakfast.

Sighing, he crossed to the coffee machine and slipped his credit card into the slot. The bitter smell made his nose itch. It was said that one of the day workers had to rip the machine apart and reprogram the biochip to force it to make a decent cup of coffee, but that was a pilot's story, and therefore automatically suspect. Still, it had to be said, the coffee was one of the few perks of the job.

Back in his chair, Allard stared out numbly into the hangar. The water vapour had dispersed into the atmosphere now, forming a mist that transfigured the spotlight beams into a gothic maze of columns and flying buttresses bracing each other against the dark. The peace would only last a few more hours, and then it would be dawn and time for the day shift to begin work.

Transpod One was due to take off empty at six thirty and meet a superspacer from Centaurii in lunar orbit. By mid-day the passengers would be unsteady in gravity once more. Transpod Two would launch at ten with a cargo of machine parts for Tycho Base. There it would exchange its load for one of ore mined from the lunar rock and arrive back at four fifteen. Transpod Three was to carry emigrants for transfer to the Mars-bound ferry, then wait for the incoming superspacer from distant Ophir bringing a cargo of zannawood, teelibean and sweet white wine. ETA on Earth: nine o'clock. Transpods Four, Five and Six were on tempo-rary standby awaiting a Cimliss shopship expected in on the local leg of its ten-planet trading cycle. Allard knew them all: their schedules, their cargoes, their des-tinations. Not the transpods, they only hoisted dead weight up and down Earth's gravitational well. No, the superspacers he knew. The real spaceships.

Allard glanced at his watch again. Christ! Two thirty already, and he still had three transpods to clean. His hands brushed over the keyboard with instinct born of habit as he aligned Transpod Four beneath the steam waldoes. They moved with febrile spider mo-tions as he scoured the soot from her sides and restored her to grace, and all the time his mind was filled with superspacers too fragile to enter gravity. He saw the stubby partridge-shape of the transpod but, whilst his hands moved by proxy over it, his eyes were filled with visions of it flying up to meet the pilots and their craft, coming and going in the heavens far above his cathedral.

Allard was good at his work, despite his dreams. Or, perhaps, because of them.

When the door behind him opened, Allard was too engrossed to notice. It was only a flicker in the flat obsidian sheet of the window that captured his attention and caused him to look up. The first thing he saw was the pilot's spacesuit. The second thing he saw was himself, reflected in the visor of the helmet the woman was carrying.

"Hi," said the pilot. "Mind if I come in?" Without waiting for an answer, she pushed the door fully open against the rusty protest of the hinges and strode across the room. While Allard tried to think of something to say the pilot looked around for somewhere to dump her helmet. The top of the coffee machine was the closest thing to hand.

"Nice setup you've got here," said the pilot in a neutral voice. "Quiet, no hassle from the bosses. Yeah, very nice." She glanced around appreciatively. "Any chance of a coffee?"

"Uh... yeah, sure. Roast, or..." "Roast's fine." The pilot wandered over to inspect the control panel, and as Allard got up he saw that she was wearing mirror-lensed sunglasses. He skin was sallow and leathery, and he couldn't guess her age. Typical pilot material.

"Just be a minute," he said, crossing to the coffee machine, suddenly very aware of every movement he was making. Please God, he whispered to himself, don't let me spill it.

"No hurry," said the pilot, moving to the window and gazing out into the void. Allard attempted to force his credit card into the slot. The pilot's helmet stared impassively down at him. By the time he turned with a cup of coffee in each hand he had regained his composure.

"We don't get many pilots in here this time of night," he said casually. "In fact, nobody ever much comes in here at night."

"I'm on short stopover," said the pilot. Her voice sounded bored, as if she had made the same small talk thousands of times before. Her eyes were invisible behind the glasses. "Arrived on the last transpod yesterday."

"The six o'clock ship? The one that met the super-spacer from Antares, the cruise ship? You mean you're a real pilot, not just a transpod jockey?"

"Yes sir, that's my baby. Full of middle aged matrons on their way back from the holiday of a lifetime, and middle-aged Antareans on their way here for the same."

"And you're really the pilot?" Allard tried to stop himself from sounding gauche and awestruck, but the pilot smiled indulgently.

"Was, kid, was. I've wangled a transfer to the

Centaurii run. Takes a good pilot to navigate in a three-sun system, least, that's what they say. Probably be dead as hell. Just like this place." She glanced around restlessly. "Where's the action around here?" she said, her mouth quirking into a grimace. "I've been sleeping solidly since groundfall last night. Woke up an hour ago, left the pilot's quarters for some kicks and couldn't find any."

"The nearest city's half an hour away," Allard said. "I mean, this is just a way station, not a place where people come for fun. I guess that's where the action is"

"You don't know for sure?" The pilot laughed: a well-practised sound carefully tailored to fit in with her manner. "What do you do for laughs then?"

"I don't get much time for that sort of thing," said Allard stiffer than he had intended. He stared out into the hangar where the transpods waited for him. Suddenly his relationship with them seemed less important than it had. Did it really matter how tawdry they really looked?

He turned so that he could see the pilot's profile. "So, how long have you been a pilot," he asked with careful casualness.

"Some time, kid, some time. Long enough to stop counting the years and start counting my blessings." She reached out and slid her fingers down the surface of the window, leaving smeared trails in their wake.

"You must have seen some sights," sighed Allard.

"Yes," said the pilot levelly, "I must have."

"I read something once about being in the Horsehead Nebula. The man who wrote it said that it was like waterfalls of fire, with all those suns shining into the dust clouds and the light bouncing back and forth. Have you ever seen it?"

"I was there on a milk run for a while."

"And was it like they say?"

"Waterfalls of fire? Yeah, I suppose it was. Quite impressive, the first time. Too bright for my liking. I'll tell you something. The writer of that piece was no pilot, that's for sure." Her eyes were mirrors and her voice was quick and bored, as if she wanted to get the old, familiar conversations over with in as short a time as possible.

"And how about out on the Rim? There are civilizations out there too, aren't there?"

"Uh-huh."

"What's it like?"

"Bleak, kid. Really bleak. Like there's nothing to see in the night sky, nothing at all. Boredom."

"But it's different nearer the centre of the galaxy, isn't it? They say there are so many stars that you can't tell the difference between night and day. They say you can't see any darkness because the stars are also dose together."

"So they say. Never bothered me enough to notice. I mean, I grew up there. Took it for granted."

Allard's eyes were round, awestruck: pupils,

dilated and dark as space. "You weren't born here on Earth?"

The pilot's lips curved into a half-smile as she replied.

"Nope, nobody in the family was, unless you go back a few generations. The family moved out as soon as the galactic lanes opened to Earth, before the travel taxes and emigration levies were imposed. This is my first trip home. No in the family's been back, except me."

"You've never been to Earth? Ever? What do you think of it?"

"Dead and forgotten, from what I've seen. All the bright young things have hitched out for better places. Nothing and no one for a passing pilot to amuse herself with in the time before take-off." The pilot cast a sideways glance at Allard, who was hanging on her every word.

"I've always wanted to be a pilot," Allard said huskily. "Always, as far back as I can remember. I used to read everything I could find about the superspacers, the pilots, the planets... It was all I ever wanted..." He raised his eyes, which prickled with frustrated tears, and stared out of the hangar. The pilot's reflection stared back at him, her mirror-glasses hiding any emotion. Any contempt. Far below them the transpod gleamed like a diamond in the spotlights.

"So what made you change your mind?" Level. Dispassionate.

"I didn't!" Allard spat through clenched teeth. "You don't know what it's like here on Earth. There's just too many people. There always have been. There isn't a choice. You do what you're told and you like it. I was lucky, at least I got a job near the spaceships."

"Come on, kid, you're in a spaceport. You can hang around, get to know the right people, get your face seen. Let them know you're keen. Someone leaves, you move into their job. Move sideways and up all the time. Sideways and up. Prove yourself for a few years and then wham! Before you know it, you're a pilot. It's easy." She smiled to herself.

Allard's eyes flickered restlessly over the confined cabin. It was still scruffy and dirty, despite his occasional half-hearted attempts to clean it. He'd never tried anything more than a cursory spit-and-polish. In his darker moments, in the early hours of the morning when he couldn't remember starting on the first transpod and couldn't conceive of finishing the last, he knew why. It would make it his cabin. It meant he knew he would never leave.

"You don't understand," he whispered. "There are just too many people. For every job there are over five hundred people qualified to..." His voice trailed away, and he waved a hand in a gesture that took in the computerised control room and the mechanised hangar beyond, with its inverted metal arms and its litter of transpods. He knew all the arguments so well that he never had to think about them. Never wanted to. "The only job worth having is a pilot's job," he sighed," and those are given away as prizes in a sweepstake."

For the first time he raised his head and looked the pilot full in the face.

"Please don't think I'm complaining," he said. "I was lucky. Completely by accident I was given a job that's almost a shadow of my dreams."

There was silence for a moment as Allard struggled with his tears.

"You're painting a dark picture, kid," the pilot said eventually. There was an edge in her voice, a tone that moved behind her words and altered their meaning, but Allard was too tired and too depressed to identify it. "You think this dump is the only planet with unemployment problems? There's lots more people where I come from, that's for sure. Same situation, though: people chosen at random to do the dirty jobs. If you're lucky you get picked as a pilot or something and you get out. If not you end up washing the transpods. Or inspecting drains. Or cleaning the computers. Or wiping the grease off the robots."

"You were lucky," said Allard.

"No," said the pilot, with a half-smile on her face. "I was unlucky. Why do you think I'm standing jawing to you and not out spending my hard-earned credits? I stared off washing transpods as well. This is a nostalgia trip for me, kid, a chance to see what I left behind. I got out. I watched, and I waited, and I took my chance. My supervisor died and I started doing his job before they could get a replacement in. So they put the replacement in my old job. And I stayed there for a lot of years. And then a new job was created when they built a new terminal on the spaceport, and I moved sideways into it before they could stop me. I moved sideways and up for a long time until I became a pilot. It took bribes, blackmail and an awful lot of time, but I made it. It's possible."

"How long?" said Allard, dry mouthed and heart thudding dully in his chest. "How long did it take you?"

The pilot didn't look at Allard, but stared out at the transpod in the overlapping circles of light. She was still smiling. "Long time, kid, like I said. You see, there's something about the atmosphere of the planet my family moved to, and the radiation from our sun, and the minerals in the soil. It took quite a few generations to make itself apparent, but the average lifespan's quite long now. It's only since my granddaddy's day that people have been living longer, but already it's having quite an effect. It took me four hundred years to do it, kid. Four hundred years, but I became a pilot like I always wanted to be." She turned her head until Allard was staring straight into the distorted image of the mirror lenses. "And I'll tell you something," she said, low and level. "It wasn't worth it."

The pilot turned away, and there were sounds of movement as she picked her helmet up off the coffee machine. Allard couldn't turn to look. He just stared out into the darkness ahead of him.

"Thanks for the drink," said the pilot. "I guess I ought to go now. Don't want to miss my flight." There was a squeak and a click as she left. Then there was silence.

Somewhere on Earth there is a boy who washes the spaceships and watches the stars.

And somewhere high in the heavens there is a pilot who laughs quietly to herself from time to time at the stories she's told. But everyone knows about pilots and their strange sense of humour. And maybe, in the solitude of her cabin, the laughter rings hollow.

LOVERS, AND OTHER STRANGERS

Amarah and I went hunting camels the day before her shuttle launched.

The frozen ground of the Steppes rang beneath the horses' hooves as we rode. Behind us the tower blocks of Star City cluttered the skyline: ahead the wilderness of Kazakhstan was broken by skeletal gantries and pitted expanses of concrete. Every few hundred yards our path Crossed one of the other avenues of open ground that linked one side of the Tyuratam Cosmodrome to the other. On our right a waist-high monkey puzzle of pipes and tubes led to a cluster of liquid hydrogen and oxygen tanks on the horizon. A battleground of blast pits and launch pads, Scarred and blackened by the heat of regular launches, stretched away on the left.

"Look, Veronique!" Amarah shouted, pointing clumsily with her gloved hand to where three mangy wolves stood watching us with hungry eyes. One took a few tentative steps as we rode by. I thought I could hear it whining, but it could have been the biting Kazakh wind as it whistled around the fuel pipes. I could tell from the way Amarah slowed down that she wanted to take a pot shot at them, but the wolves around the Cosmodrome were notoriously wary of people who looked as if they could protect themselves. Besides, unlike the camels, their flesh was tough and their pelts almost worthless on the black market.

By the time the sun had fallen to the horizon we had found no camels and ridden so far across Tyuratam that we could see the current launch pad. The Energiya rocket was already bathed in lights, and even from a few miles away we could see the frantic prelaunch preparations. Amarah's face was a mask of joyful pride as she gazed up at the Buran shuttle, which clung to the booster assembly like a lovesick peasant. She looked pure, strong, as if she was posing for a painting in the Stalin-approved school of Patriotic Realism. She looked beautiful.

When the light began to fail we started back for home – or the place I had been calling home for three weeks whilst waiting for the launch and falling in love with Amarah. I still found it hard to believe that a place like Star City existed. For a while, of course, neither could anybody else. Soviet press releases had always referred to it as the Baikonur Cosmodrome in a vain attempt to confuse Western intelligence agencies, although it was hundreds of kilometres from Baikonur. Now the press releases were using the UN launch as a selling point, trying to attract commercial interest in the launch site. One place: two histories. It's a funny old world.

As we reached the outskirts of the town Amarah reined in her horse and motioned for me to do the same. I started to speak, but she shushed me.

Something moved in the shadows close to a

concrete blast shelter. A large, blunt head appeared near to the ground, Cropping at the sparse grasses. As the camel moved forward its sinuous neck emerged into the horizontal rays of sunset, followed by a lumpy body set atop ungainly and splayed legs. Another Camel followed it out into the light, and then another. Amarah reached into her jacket and pulled out her heavy Makarov pistol. The lead camel, scenting something new in the air, raised its head. Its eyes were large, brown, and ringed with lashes. It seemed to be looking directly at me. Amarah raised the gun and squinted along it at the camel's head. After a pause long enough for me to Count the Sores on its skin, Amarah lowered the gun. The camel looked away, and continued browsing. The rest of the herd slowly followed as it moved incuriously away.

I looked across at Amarah. "Cash on four legs," I sighed. "You always tell me how underpaid the space industry is compared with Europe."

"Don't, Veronique," she murmured. "I just couldn't

"Blinovitch will be pissed off. He's already got orders in for the meat."

"Blinovitch can go screw himself," she said. "Tomorrow's a big day. I keep thinking: André and I are going to be the first people ever to meet an alien race! I don't want to spoil it by killing." She paused, and smiled. "Not even a camel."

We rode back in silence, but by the time we

reached the small cooperative where the horses were stabled we had achieved some kind of tacit understanding. As we walked across the squares and wide *prospekts* of Star City, emptier now that the workers were preparing for the launch, I felt Amarah's hand slip into mine. By the time we had reached her room in one of the many apartment blocks we were smiling at each other, and by the time we were in her bed it was as if we had never argued.

In the afterglow of passion, as condensation trickled down the windows, I reached across Amarah for my tape recorder.

"Do you mind?"

"What the hell," she said, smiling contentedly and nodding towards the device. "I know you have to. And we wouldn't have met if it hadn't been for that thing."

She was right, of course. As *Le Monde*'s Russian stringer I usually spent most of my time reporting on back-stabbing in Parliament and drive-by shootings in St Petersburg. When the UN announced that their representative was being flown to the orbital rendezvous with the mysterious aliens in the off-again on-again Russian shuttle Buran, I had been on the first flight out to Star City. Chance of a lifetime.

Amarah gazed up at me as I supported myself on one elbow. Her hand slowly ran down my side. Her smile was beautiful: it was the first thing I had noticed when I had interviewed her: the pilot who would take

André Ferrand to the Cimliss spacecraft. It had broken my journalistic concentration and made me watch her as a person, made me aware of the way she smelled, the way her hair moved, the curve of her neck into her shoulder.

"So, Amarah Polovska," I said, pressing the REC-ORD button, "how do you feel on the evening before your launch?"

She reached up and pulled me down towards her. "I thought you were supposed to be an investigative journalist?" she whispered.

The dictaphone went on recording, but we weren't talking.

Although I felt, and was usually treated, like one of the launch team, I was watching alongside selected representatives of the world's press from the observation lounge as the shuttle climbed into the pure blue sky. Amarah's calm, professional voice was being piped through into the lounge. Blinovitch, the big, bearded UN representative and local black- marketeer, kept feeding us tea spiked with vodka. There seemed to be no problems with the booster separations. Long after the fragile metal container vanished from sight its plume hung suspended in the still air. And then, just as a stable orbit was about to be achieved, I heard André's voice in the background.

"Polovska! Look at that!"

"*Bozhe moi!* They're beautiful."

"Ground Control," André said, more formally,

"we have visual contact with the Cimliss Craft." He sounded as though he knew posterity would be listening. "They're... ah... reddish, and covered with... ah... extrusions..."

"Spikes," Amarah murmured. "Spikes, and there must be 20 of them. Size difficult to estimate..."

"But they're big."

"But they're big, and —"

"Buran," the calm, professional voice of Ground Control broke in, "please check your position."

Amarah read out a string of numbers."

"Buran, please confirm that position." I felt a slow shiver pass up my spine. Blinovitch glanced over at me and smiled in reassurance, but I could see that he was concerned. A ripple of unease passed through the crowd. Journalists spoke urgently to camera or to dictaphone.

Amarah read another string of numbers back: they sounded identical to me, and I could hear the worry in her voice.

"Buran, we have a slight problem. You appear to have drifted slightly off course. Please check your attitude control thrusters."

"We show fuel states normal, and all failsafes operative," Amarah responded instantly. She must have already anticipated the request.

"Buran, radar shows that a normal orbit can be achieved, but you'll be about a hundred kilometres from where the Cimliss asked for you to be. I'm sure they won't mind." Irony tinged Ground Control's voice. "We'll ask them to come and pick you up."

"No problem, Ground Control," Amarah said, relieved. "Please tell them —"

There was a sudden burst of static, and then nothing but the hum of a dead carrier wave. I wasn't a technician, I had never seen a launch before, so I didn't know whether this was standard practice or not, but the sudden flurry of activity in the observation suite and the questions which Ground Control were barking, and which neither Amarah nor André were answering, made me worry. The ground suddenly felt as if it had vanished from beneath my feet. Blinovitch glanced towards me, frowning, and said something, but I was insulated from the rest of the world in a hot little bubble of my own, and I could not hear him.

I don't remember anything between then and when I burst through the doors to the cold, cavernous room they called Ground Control with Blinovitch trying to hold me back. People in jeans and T-shirts were standing around, doing nothing. I was the first and last of the journalists in, and that was only because my relationship with Amarah had spread during the weeks of our relationship to include Blinovitch and the rest of the technicians and operators. The press were outsiders; I was almost family.

There was no agitation. There was no confusion. Just bewilderment and a terrible sense of finality. Some people were attempting to get through to the UN or the

Commonwealth Space Organization offices at Moscow or Alma-Ata on the telephones and announce the news, but from what I could hear of their curses the exchanges were continually busy.

I threaded my way through the rows of consoles until I stood before the main screen. It was displaying what I guessed to be a radar picture of the area where... where the Buran should have been. There was nothing but a blurred area now, dispersing and fading as I watched, and a mass of signals nearby which must have been the Cimliss spacecraft.

I felt like the picture: blurred, almost lost in static. Blinovitch placed his hands on my shoulders. I wanted to ask him what had happened, but the words jammed in my throat. I wanted to scream, or to cry, but everything was trapped inside me.

"One moment the shuttle was there," he said from behind me, his voice a cheap cigarette rasp in my ear. I could feel him shrug. "The next moment, it wasn't. They got their orbital insertion wrong. A problem with the booster, little bit more thrust in an unexpected direction, it happens. Not usually important. Don't know what happened."

"They were destroyed," one of the computer operators said behind me. "The aliens, they are invading!"

"It must have been an accident," someone else yelled from across the room. "A collision..."

As the argument began, I slipped away. Part of me knew I should be interviewing, reporting, acting as

Le Monde's person on the spot. A spot, at least. The rest of me just wanted to lash out at anybody who tried to stop me curling up in the observation lounge with one of Blinovitch's bottles of black-market vodka and watching the end of the world.

In the end, it didn't matter. Whatever reports I could have filed would probably have been duplicated 20 times over by the massed ranks of the press. The alien Cimliss made every page of every paper and every minute of air time for the next few days. Wars were ignored and economies neglected as they apologized for the loss of our shuttle, claiming that its unexpected course correction had made it drift into the path of whatever mighty engines pushed their ships across space. "Like a pigeon sucked into a propeller," the British tabloid press had said in a grisly, but apt, phrase. I almost passed out when I first heard it, but frequent repetition dulled the pain.

The Cimliss went on to suggest that perhaps it would be better if they landed, and did so, in Ecuador. I sat for most of that day and the following night watching CNN with Blinovitch and some of the technicians in Ground Control. Blinovitch had broken out his last crate of vodka. "After all," he said, "it's history."

In what we assumed at the time was just the turmoil of the moment, the newsreaders referred to the tragic explosion of the American shuttle soon after launch. There was a near riot amongst the technicians. Blinovitch threatened to rip the wire out of the plug if they didn't shut up and listen.

An hour later, after on-the-spot footage of the Cimliss spacecraft nestling amongst the trees and a live broadcast from the American President, CNN circled back briefly to the Buran. They were still referring to it as American, but this time they mentioned in passing that the French Government had claimed not only André Ferrand but also Amarah Polovska as French citizens.

Soon after that a technician who had been listening to the World Service on his radio heard the BBC talking about an accident involving two British astronauts on the UN diplomatic mission launched from Kazakhstan.

We just looked at each other, aghast. They had been our friends, and we felt as if we were losing them all over again.

It was two hours later that Sky News reported new information. By now the Cimliss had invited all heads of Government to meet them, but all we were interested in was mentions of the Buran. This time it was the Japanese Prime Minister who, in a speech to his people, referred in passing to the tragic deaths of a Japanese diplomat and a Japanese pilot in an accident.

Blinovitch took a telephone call—the first time that anybody had bothered to get in touch with us, despite our frantic attempts to report the disaster to Moscow and Alma-Ata and Geneva. It was Itar-Tass, the news agency, wanting biographies of the Russian

Cosmonauts Amarah Polovska and André Ferrand. I was furious, not so much for Ferrand, my countryman, but for Amarah. I knew how much she valued her hard-won Moldovan heritage. Had valued.

Blinovitch took me aside. "Something's going on, Veronique," he murmured. On the TV screen behind him the tiny silhouettes of eagles soared against a spiky orange metal background whilst a newsreader tried to keep up with his teleprompter.

"It's just the confusion..." I told him, but even as I spoke I knew that he was right.

"It's more than confusion, it's those things." He pointed to the TV. "Somehow, getting caught in their wake has... I don't know... unravelled Amarah and André. Those ships must use some sort of mechanism that warps space. It's warped them as well." He tapped the side of his head. "They've been spread out across the universe of the mind. They're just a symbol now. They belong to all of us."

"Bullshit," I snapped, close to the edge of hysteria. He was drunk. Drunk and maudlin.

He began to cry. I reached out and touched his shoulder.

"She was my sister," he wept, "I was so proud of her. So proud of my little Amarah."

I couldn't believe what I was hearing. My hand fell away from him. He wiped a sleeve across his eyes.

"My only sister..." he continued. "My girlfriend," said a voice behind Blinovitch. Rutskoi, one of the backup cosmonauts, came up behind him. He too was crying. "We were to be married," he continued. "When she landed. And now... What is there left?"

I backed away, shaking my head. The ground seemed to be rocking under my feet, and I could feel a strange buzzing sensation creeping through my head. Everything seemed to be moving slowly, dreamily. I don't think either of them noticed me stagger away; they were too busy consoling each other over their loss.

All around me people were crying. One of the babushkas from the canteen was wailing over the death of her son, André. I picked up the last bottle of vodka and left. -

Walking through the empty early morning streets towards my apartment block I could see the flicker of televisions behind every set of curtains. People watching history. I took a long swig from the bottle. As my head tipped back I could see the stars cold and haughty, hanging above me, above all of us, changeless and eternal. Suddenly I needed to hear her again, just to reassure myself that she was real. Or that I was.

The weight of the tape recorder was dragging my pocket down. Last night we had made love, and then rewound the tape and listened to ourselves, and then made love again, excited by the voyeurism. It was all I had left, apart from memories. No photographs, no letters. Nothing of Amarah except for the most precious thing that we had shared.

I took the recorder from my pocket and weighed

it in my hand. It was my proof. She had been my lover. A scattering of raindrops sluiced across my face. I threw it away, and watched it tumble over and over until the darkness swallowed it up.

DEPENDENCE DAY

By Andy Lane and Justin Richards

By now, the Earth Empire was in tatters. With the connivance of Empress Leabie Inyathi Forrester, planets had seceded left, right and centre. Alien governments had taken advantage of the change in policy to break treaties and change alliances, effectively isolating Earth from the galactic trade routes. The big corporations had all withdrawn their funding from the planet, wrecking Earth's economy at a stroke. The only people on Earth were those who either could not or would not leave. Leabie Inyathi Forrester - Divine Empress, Glory of the Empire, Ruler of the High Court, Lord of the Inner and Outer Worlds, High Admiral of the Galactic· Fleets, Lord General of the Six Armies and Defender of the Earth - was reduced to abject poverty in the ruins of what used to be her Summer Palace...

from *The Gutter to the Stars: A History of the Forrester Family*
by Tranlis Difarallio

One of the tapestries was lying in a crumpled heap on

the floor, and the wall on which it had hung was cracked open. Through the crack Thandiwe Forrester could see grey clouds and the ruined tops of the nearby buildings. A breeze nuzzled her cheek, bringing with it coolness and the smell of smoke. For a moment she thought she could hear crying in the darkness outside. Or singing.

"How do you think it happened?" she asked her sister.

"There was some fighting near the Palace a few days ago," Gugwani said. "Some of the local gangs got too close, and the guards had to open fire." She reached out to touch the blackened edge of the crack, and the material crumbled beneath her fingers. "I think a couple of shots missed and hit the outside of the wall. I found it like this yesterday."

Thandiwe looked around, down the sloping corridor towards the state rooms and the great ballroom. "We should tell someone. Mother, or one of the guards. The gangs might be able to get in through here! They're always hanging around the Palace. It ought to be repaired."

"Don't be such an idiot." Gugwani experimentally pulled a chunk of wall away, widening the crack. "I bet I could squeeze through here."

"Gugwani, I don't think -"

With a sudden, decisive motion, Gugwani pressed herself against the crack and began to squirm through. Flakes of marble pattered to the floor, and

Thandiwe could smell burning, like a fading ghost of a fire.

"Don't - don't go!" she cried.

"They never let us go outside," her sister gasped as she forced herself through the gap. I just want to see what it's like. I'll be back in a moment, I promise. Maybe I'll find us some food - there must be someone out here who has some and wouldn't mind giving it to me. I am a princess, after all." She vanished from sight. For a few seconds Thandiwe could hear the scuff of her shoes against the ground, then there was silence.

"Gugwani? Gugwani, please come back! Can you hear me?"

She waited for almost five minutes, calling occasionally to her sister and growing more and more terrified, before she ran for help.

*   *   *

Tranlis Difarallio's ship picked up the first signs of Earth's fate when he was still five light years away.

He was dreaming of the Forresters when it happened: an endless line of dark-skinned men and women standing in the shadows, each with right hand on the shoulder of the one in front, the meagre illumination highlighting their sharp cheek- bones and the strong lines of their jaws. Each of them was wearing different clothes from the others - he spotted spacesuits ranging from primitive to baroque, as well as fatigues of various colours and standards of cleanliness, cybernetic harnesses and flowing velvet robes - but each was somehow staring at him through the same pair of eyes. Not accusing, not angry, not supportive, but just... wary. Just watching.

"I'm intercepting some interesting snippets from historical Earth Empire news bulletins, Tranlis," his ship said, its asexual voice insinuating itself, quiet and reassuring, into his dreams. "Electromagnetic radiation: barely above the back ground threshold. They're time-stamped just under five years ago. Would you like to see them?"

Tranlis opened his eyes and stretched in his womb-chair. The chair stretched back, pushing against his spine and rubbing itself seductively against the nape of his neck. The parade of Forresters backed away from him and into the shadows. "What makes them so different from the rest of the broadcasts you've been monitoring on the way here?" he asked muzzily.

The ship shrugged in his mind. 'revolution, the assassination of the Divine Empress, the new Emperor and the rebel- lion, the coronation of Leabie Inyathi Forrester as Empress. Dramatic stuff. Given the reason we're going to Earth in the first place, I thought...'' It let the sentence hang.

Tranlis considered for a moment. The ship probably had a point - the more information he had, the better he could finish the job he had come to do - but... 'Surely we've got all that stuff from the fastline transmissions of *The Empire Today*. They covered the whole mess and transmitted the reports in real time to the rest of the Empire. It's all recorded in your memory, ready for when I write the final chapters of the history."

"Yes, I know that," the ship said without a trace of condescension. "But these are local transmissions - internal Imperial communications between the Empress's Winter Palace and her Summer Palace on Earth, mobilization orders for her troops, local news updates: messages broadcast from one point to another that just kept on going, weakened by distance but still decipherable. This is the news as it actually happened, whereas the material you downloaded into my memory before we left Omphalos Prime is, if you'll forgive me, predigested pap written by the winning side."

"Point taken." Tranlis thought for a moment, letting his chair knead the tension of sudden waking from the back of his neck. "OK, save anything you think might be of value and I'll look through it later." He grimaced. "Ninety-nine point nine per cent of it will be a tedious waste of time, you realize?"

"Ninety-nine point nine per cent of everything is a tedious waste of time," the ship replied smoothly, "but the important bits wouldn't be important without them."

"Who's writing this history?" Tranlis muttered.

"That's a rhetorical question," the ship countered. "You are, of course. A better question might be, who should be writing this history?"

Tranlis bit his tongue.

As they swept through the dark reaches of space towards Earth, past deserted star systems and abandoned colony worlds, Tranlis scanned the research material for his final few chapters. Virtual screens floated around his head, and his attention flickered from one to another, collating facts, speculations and theories. He had tied together the entire history of the family, from their beginnings in Africa through to the thirtieth century. All that was left was to review the lives of Roslyn Forrester and her sister Leabie, and he was finished.

He leant back in the womb-chair and let his eyes refocus beyond the floating screens while he marshalled his thoughts. His gaze moved between the objects displayed on stands against the bulkhead: the ceremonial Xhosa club wielded by a tribal Forrester before the family even changed their name; the small robotic vehicle in which Jack Forrester had left Pellucidar Station on his exploration of the galaxy; the few remaining fragments of the escape pod within which Jon Forrester had returned to New Zion. None of them really registered; his mind was too full of the end of the story. The end to which he was so close.

Roslyn was the family misfit, a rebel who had left the comfort of the Baronial mansion on Io to become a lowly Adjudicator on Earth. Tranlis had already made extensive notes on this bizarre compulsion towards law enforcement within the Forrester family, but he still didn't understand why it was buried so deeply in their psyche. Perhaps Leabie could tell him. Perhaps she could also tell him why, in the midst of a massive and mysterious conspiracy, Roslyn Forrester had gone missing, listed as a traitor to the Empire along with her partner Chris Cwej. Leabie, meanwhile, had prospered as a debutant in the court of the Empress. The "official" history was confused about what happened next, although it appeared that Roslyn had returned to Earth and helped her sister organize a rebellion against the increasingly harsh rule of the Empire. Skimming through the contemporaneous messages that the ship had intercepted didn't help - nobody at the time seemed to know what was going on either. By the time Earth emerged from the fog of historical confusion, Roslyn Forrester and the Empress were both dead and Leabie was the new Empress.

And within five years she had dismantled the Empire. Wholesale. With a few deft signatures and the wielding of a royal seal, every planet in the Empire was suddenly granted independence. Even the ones that didn't want it.

And only Leabie knew why.

"We're approaching Earth," the ship interrupted. 'Shall I take us in to land?"

"Yes please." Tranlis looked past the swarm of screens. "What does it look like?"

'see for yourself."

The ship swept the virtual screens away from

Tranlis's head and replaced them with a representation of what was outside the ship: a shadowed disc against the sea of stars with the sun emerging from behind it like a great gem atop a ring of gold. It struck him how dark the planet itself was. He was used to the worlds of the new federations and hegemonies that were springing up in the wake of the Empire, glowing with jewelled clusters of cities and industrial areas whose edges expanded even as one watched-. "Is there... is there any sign of life?" he asked.

"That depends what you mean by "life". I'm not discerning any signs of power transmission - none of the generators are working - but there are bonfires and campfires scattered across the face of the planet, each surrounded by crowds of humans numbering from a few tens to a few hundred. Oh, and I'm discerning too many automated distress beacons to count." The ship sniffed. "Probably irradiators and tech brains with their own internal power supplies, abandoned by their owners when the Overcities fell. We need not concern ourselves with them.".

"No humans transmitting at all?"

There was no perceptible pause while the ship scanned. "None. The planet has been all but forsaken since the Empire fell apart. Nobody visits here any more. I would expect that, after five years, anyone calling out into the darkness hoping for an answer would have given up."

"I expect you're right. You usually are." Tranlis

hesitated. "You said "bonfires and campfires". Pardon my ignorance, but what's the difference?"

"The campfires are for cooking food - they're the ones with only a few tens of people or fewer around them. The bonfires are the ones with a few hundred people around them. They appear to be for burning people alive."

Tranlis gazed again at the growing bulk of Earth. "Descent to barbarism and savagery. Religious cults and would-be saviours springing up all over the planet. Sacrifices to the gods who have abandoned them. It's happened before."

"But not to Earth," the ship said, echoing his unspoken thoughts. "Never to Earth."

"What about aliens?" Tranlis asked, suppressing a. shudder. "There was a large non-human population here before the Fall, mainly concentrated in the Under-towns."

"You remember I mentioned campfires?"

"Are you trying to tell me they're cooking the aliens?"

"Where do you think the food is coming from? What's laughingly referred to as soil on Earth is completely bereft of nutrients, even if they had the seeds to plant, and the remnants of humanity have nothing to trade for food, even if any trader wanted to waste their time coming here."

"But..." He shook his head in disbelief. "They're cooking the aliens?"

"Just another kind of animal - probably the only kind of animal the planet has left, thinking about it. It's very obvious that only humans are congregating together around the campfires and bonfires. The aliens are slinking around in the shadows, or hiding in the wrecks of the Overcities. Some are moving very rapidly, pursued by large groups of humans. Except..."

Tranlis glanced at the virtual screen; the edges of the planet had drifted beyond its boundaries. The ship's curving path to the surface had put them in a position where the sun was illuminating a quarter of the globe: a shattered jigsaw of grey and brownish-red. He could see no trace of the oceans that had once occupied most of its surface. "Except what?"

"Except I'm picking up..." Unusually, the ship paused again. "I'm now picking up what appear to be alien ships on the Earth's surface. Lots of them."

The virtual screen suddenly accelerated sickeningly towards the planet. Tranlis jerked upright and grabbed for the edges of his chair, half convinced for a moment that the ship was heading for a crash-landing. The chair held his hands comfortingly and tried to ease him back.

"Sorry about that, Tranlis."

The screen juddered to a halt, and Tranlis found himself looking down on a rubble-strewn plain. Weeds grew through cracks in the surface, and in three or four places there were gaps through which Tranlis could see the glittering waters of an underground river.

"I'm holding us in orbit while I check these out," the ship said. "I've picked out several hundred of them, scattered around the globe. They were screened, which is why I couldn't discern them until now."

In the centre of the picture Tranlis could make out what appeared to be an alien spacecraft. Judging by the thousands of humans crowded around it, the ship must have been huge. Its surface was spiky and it was coloured an autumnal orange tinged with green. It was difficult to see at that extreme magnification, but Tranlis thought he could make out dark openings around the ship's hull. The crowds were clustering at those points.

"What's going on?" he asked, standing up and stretching.

"I wish I knew," the ship replied. "I can discern the ships, but I can't discern any alien life forms in or around them. Odd."

"I don't recognize the configuration." He wandered towards the virtual screen stretched across the front of the room. On a sill beside it stood a display stand, and on the stand was a ceremonial Xhosa club, turned from real wood, smoothed and polished millennia ago. He stroked the backs of his fingers along it.

"Neither do I. It's certainly not any race I've come across before, unless they've radically redesigned their ships. Would you still like me to land?"

He thought for a moment, then said, "Yes. Have you located the Empress's Summer Palace yet?"

As the virtual screen blurred, and the scene of the alien ship receded like Tranlis's dream, the ship replied, "I have. There are life forms inside, but I cannot tell whether any of them is the Empress or not. You're taking a chance, Tranlis."

"Tell me about it. The last thing we heard, she had returned to the Summer Palace when the Empire collapsed. There were sporadic reports for some time saying that she was still living there. I have neither the time nor the resources to search the entire planet for her: we'll try there, ask around and, if we can't find her, leave. I can finish the history without her: I'd just rather not."

"Accepted and agreed," the ship said. "There's a space I can land in near the Palace."

A sudden thought struck Tranlis. "How close is the nearest of the alien ships?"

"A few miles." . The ship paused, and Tranlis thought he could feel a half-smile in his mind. "Given the number of them around, you don't have to wander far before you stumble across one of them.".

The background hum, of the ship's operations, a noise Tranlis had long since ceased to hear, suddenly altered pitch slightly and made itself obvious again. A section of the bulkhead puckered and drew back like a curtain to reveal a dark, star-scattered sky. Air scented with wood smoke wafted into the ship.

"We've arrived," it said.

*   *   *

The Divine Empress, once Glory of the Empire, previous Ruler of the High Court, prior Lord of the Inner and Outer Worlds, quondam High Admiral of the Galactic Fleets, former Lord General of the Six Armies and past Defender of the Earth, Leabie Inyathi Forrester, gazed blindly around the familiar ruins of her throne room. Her courtiers stood by, powerless to comfort her. Her tears blinded her to the fallen pillars, the ripped draperies, the cracked marble flagstones, the fallen chandeliers. Through the blurred vision of her grief, the throne room glittered with diamonds and her courtiers were once again dressed in their full regalia, rather than tatters and rags.

"Are you -" she began, but her words caught in her throat and she sobbed silently for a moment. In front of her throne - a metal chair covered with a velvet curtain that had seen better days - the Commander in Chief of her Elite Landsknechte Ceremonial Guard hefted his blaster rifle uncomfortably. "Are you absolutely sure? Is there no doubt at all in your mind?"

"Your most puissant Majesty," he stammered, "I am sure." He blinked and looked away. "I have no hesitation in conveying the tragic news that your daughter is dead."

"What was Gugwani doing outside the Palace?" Leabie shouted suddenly. "You should have had men guarding her! You should have been protecting her!"

"Your Majesty!" The Commander in Chief's outrage momentarily overcame his habitual caution. "Three of my best men were assigned to her at all times, but she is... was… wilful! If she wished to leave the Palace, there was little my men could do to stop her." "What happened?" she whispered, subsiding. "There will be no punishment. We know you did your best."

He sighed heavily. "The first thing my men knew was when your daughter Thandiwe told them her sister had climbed through a crack in the wall and hadn't come back. I sent two men through the window after her. They found her at the end of the old bridge that used to connect the Palace with the plaza and called to her to stop, but she called back that she was starving and she was going to find food -"

Leabie shook her head. "The poor girl," she whispered. "We have told her so many times that we must endure this hardship. Our subjects... our subjects have less to eat even than we do. There is no food to be found out there."

"We tried to tell her that, your Majesty, but she would not listen. Twenty men were dispatched to intercept her, but by the time they caught up..." He fumbled to a halt, his head slumping.

Leabie leant forward and touched him beneath the chin with her forefinger, raising his head again. "Continue."

'she was running across the plaza outside the Palace when the cannibal gang caught her. They had been hiding beneath the flagstones, in hollowed-out spaces, waiting for one of your courtiers to pass." He straightened his shoulders. "They would never have dared attack a Landsknechte Marine, of course."

"We have no doubts about your men's abilities," Leabie murmured.

"They sprang out on her before my men could intervene. There were twenty, perhaps thirty of them. They dragged her across the plaza by her hair." He leant forward, not wanting to distress the rest of the courtiers. "They prefer not to bruise the flesh of their victims, I understand."

Leabie nodded, feeling grief twist her heart.

The Commander in Chief would not meet her gaze. Instead his eyes flicked nervously from side to side. "Mindful of... of your Majesty's instructions that neither you nor either of your daughters were ever to be captured alive by the cannibal gangs..."

She knew what he was going to say. She wanted to reach out and stop his mouth; she wanted to have him, and anyone else who might tell her what they had done, killed and their heads strung together on a banner across the Palace gateway as a warning to all who might bring her bad news, but she didn't. She listened to his words as her grief squirmed inside her like something alive.

"Mindful, as I say, of your often-repeated instructions, we

... we..." He swallowed. "Killed her. With the last few

ergs of energy left in our blaster power packs."

"And." The word seemed to spill from her lips without conscious volition.

The Commander in Chief was at a loss. "And what, your Majesty?"

"And what happened next?"

He looked around at the faces of the scrawny, grimy courtiers. None of them would look at him. "And then the cannibal gangs ate her cooked remains, there and then, your Majesty. But at least -"

"But at least she was not alive to feel it." A great weight was pressing her down in the throne. "You did... what was required of you. Go now. We will ensure that you and the troops who carried out this... this noble deed... will have double rations at the next meal. Whenever that happens to be."

"Your Majesty is most gracious." He backed away as fast as he could while still preserving decorum, stumbling slightly on the sloping floor. When Leabie had ordered the Palace's null-grav generators turned off slowly five years before, allowing the Palace to come to rest on the surface of the Earth, she had tried to pick the flattest surface she could find and trusted to the weight of the Palace to flatten whatever irregularities remained. Unfortunately, the Palace had been built for decoration rather than strength, and the ruins of the Undertown beneath it had cracked its immense base into several pieces.

"And our other daughter?" she asked.

He stopped. "Your daughter Thandiwe is unharmed, your Majesty. I have doubled her guard."

"A wise move."

As he left the throne room, the features of her courtiers - her maids, grooms, butlers, pages and ceremonial guards - all blurred together into one gaunt, wild-eyed face, staring at her with eyes starved of hope. She dug her fingernails into the velvet covering her metal throne and stifled a scream. She must not cry. She must preserve the dignity that befitted her rank. They had nothing else! They depended on her!

One face stood out from the throng: a plump face sur- rounded by hair that was brown rather than grey, and styled rather than matted. Leabie tried to focus on it. Surely it wasn't one of her courtiers? If it was then he must have been stealing food for months to keep himself going, and she would have him flogged before banishing him beyond the Palace walls. Anger sharpened her eyesight, and as she stared harder at the newcomer she knew with chilling certainty that she had never seen him before. An outsider! In her Palace!

"Who are you?" she asked in the most regal voice she could muster. "And where have you come from?"

The stranger stepped forward, and her courtiers drew back from him. His clothes were woven from a fine ceramic thread, and shimmered like ripples on water. Leabie had not seen clothes like those since -

Since she had destroyed the Empire.

Tardily, her Elite Landsknechte Ceremonial

Guards rushed to surround the man, aiming their weapons at his head. Leabie hoped he couldn't see the power indicators: half of them weren't even lit.

"My name is Tranlis Difarallio," he said. "I am from the planet Omphalos Prime."

"We used to own Omphalos Prime," she said haughtily, still holding back her grief behind walls as fragile as those of her Palace. "We remember it as being a cold, purple world."

He smiled. "Indeed it is, your Majesty."

"And do they still talk of our enlightened rule there?"

His smile broadened. "Indeed they do, your Majesty. They talk of little else."

Leabie relaxed slightly. He was deferential, but not unduly so, and he had a sense of humour. He must have known that she had no real power, but he was willing to go along with the illusion of it. She gestured to the guards to stand down.

Her mind - still active, despite the charades and the play- acting - pored over the question of why he was there. She had nothing to give, no goods and none of whatever currency they were using in the galaxy now, so whatever he was doing on Earth it had nothing to do with trade. Earth in general, and the Palace in particular, had seen its fair share of sightseers in the few months after she had finally and irrevocably destroyed the Empire, but they had dropped off quickly, and she had seen none for several years. Besides, he didn't carry himself like a sightseer.

In fact, he looked more like an academic. Another academic.

"You are writing a history of the Empire," she stated. She was pleased to see his eyebrows rise slightly in astonishment, but she maintained her regal impassivity. "Others, we believe, have done the same. They came and asked us questions. We refused to answer them." Well, except for the last few who had offered food in return, but she wasn't going to admit to that.

"I have read their books," Difarallio said. "Many of them described you, your Majesty, but none had the words to describe your great beauty and serenity."

She couldn't help smiling, despite the sharp agony of Gugwani's loss. He was impertinent, this one. Perhaps she would help him, after all. Even if he didn't offer food. "We will not tell you why we destroyed the Empire," she warned. "There are some secrets we must keep."

"My lady, I am not writing a history of the Empire," he said, holding his hands wide to indicate his honesty. Leabie didn't fail to notice the subtle shift from "your Majesty" to "my lady". He was giving notice that the formalities had been observed and now it was time to discuss business.

"I am (engaged in writing a more personal history - one of the Forrester family."

Now it was her eyebrows that rose in astonishment. "But - who would be interested?"

He shrugged. "Your family has followed a very interesting path. I have been able to trace them back as far as a large city named Tower Hamlets here on Earth - perhaps on this very spot - before spaceflight became a reality. They were dependent on the government of the time for food. Each succeeding generation has been more self-reliant, more powerful. For a thousand years the Forresters have gradually expanded, amassing more wealth and more power." He wasn't looking at her any more, he was looking through her and seeing something beyond her imagining. "Just think of it," he continued, his voice rising, "Forrester after Forrester, each living and dying but each improving the lot of the family by one precious little bit: a continuous heritage starting from a slum and ending up -" His eyes suddenly focused back on reality as his arms spread out to indicate the throne room.

"Ending up in another slum," Leabie said dryly. "We can see the appeal of such a history. Didn't they used to call them "cautionary tales"?"

He lowered his arms. "I only have one chapter left to complete," he said in a calmer voice. "The one covering your father and mother, yourself and your sister, and your daughters. If you will permit me to stay for a few days and ask you some questions. I have..." An embarrassed ex pression crossed his face. "I have some food on my ship, some supplies l was bringing for you. I realize times are hard."

"I will answer your questions," Leabie said,

deliberately switching to a less formal mode of address and rising from her throne. "If...If you will tell me of my ancestors. I would like to hear their stories while you hear mine."

Tranlis nodded gratefully. "I will go and fetch the supplies I brought."

He turned to go, but Leabie stopped him with a gesture. "No. Tonight you will eat with us. If you wish to hear my story, you should experience first-hand what it is like to live here, in this cold, draughty palace, day after day - this Palace that used to float so elegantly above the rest of the Overcities, but now sits unsteadily upon their ruins, and upon the ruins of the Undertowns beneath them. You will sleep here as well, in the damp, listening to the songs and the screams from outside the Palace walls. When you have finished asking your questions, then you may leave, and you may leave your supplies behind."

*   *   *

From her position on the troubadours" balcony, over-looking the shadowed banqueting room, Thandiwe had a perfect view of the stranger. His shining clothes singled him out from the rest of the courtiers at the bare table. He sat next to her mother, the Empress, and he listened politely but not deferentially as she talked. Thandiwe could just about make out what her mother was saying. She was talking about Roslyn, the aunt

Thandiwe had only met briefly but felt strangely close to. Her mother didn't talk very much about Aunt Roslyn - in fact, she looked uncomfortable and changed the subject whenever Thandiwe tried to raise it. Thandiwe concentrated on trying to make out what her mother was saying.

If she concentrated really, really hard, she might even be able to stop thinking about Gugwani.

"Roslyn was always a rebellious child. I remember she ran away from father's Palace on Io, oh, must be half a dozen times before she finally left for good. He knew every time, of course - she had two sets of bodyguards, the set she was supposed to see every day and lose when she ran away, and a second set who she never saw anµ who stayed with her even after she ran away. She always came back, though. Always - except for the last time. Except when she joined the Adjudicators."

"Did your father let her keep the bodyguards then?" the stranger asked.

Thandiwe's mother shook her head. "He did for a while, but she kept arresting them for loitering and throwing them in jail. It all got too embarrassing for father. All the court circulars reported it. He eventually withdrew them." She looked away. "Perhaps, if he hadn't -"

Thandiwe's mother was interrupted by the arrival of the servants from the shadows. They were each carrying a steaming platter of some unidentified meat.

The smell wafted up towards where Thandiwe was crouching, and she felt her nostrils prickling and her mouth flooding with saliva at the smell. She hadn't seen food like that for as long as she could remember.

"I distinctly asked you not to fetch the supplies from your ship," Thandiwe's mother snapped at the stranger.

He frowned. "And I obeyed your wishes, your Majesty. "This food isn't from my ship, I assure you." He sniffed appreciatively. "But it smells good. I'm surprised - I had expected there to be problems with the food supply here." A faint shadow of unease crossed his face. "It isn't...I mean, it is animal meat, isn't it? Not - not anything else."

"We're not cannibals," Thandiwe's mother said grimly. Thandiwe felt a stab of sudden guilt pierce her heart. "And I refuse to countenance the eating of aliens." She turned to one of the servants. "Rachellia, where did this meat come from?"

Thandiwe liked Rachellia, a gaunt, blonde woman who always had a small treat for her and for Gugwani in the Palace kitchens. She shuffled closer to the edge of the balcony as Rachellia stepped forward.

"There are aliens, your majesty. Alien spaceships, giving out food. They say that many alien races are working together to ship food to Earth so that we don't starve. They're just giving it away. Just giving it away. Isn't it wonderful?"

Thandiwe shivered, and she didn't know why.

*   *   *

They ate well that evening. There was a. suspicion, a wariness about the court, but food was food and they were starving. By the end of the meal they were intoxicated despite the absence of alcohol. Only Thandiwe and her mother ate little, their hearts and consciences still heavy from the loss of Gugwani.

And that night Thandiwe dreamt for the first time in years.

She had suffered nightmares, of course. Almost every time she slept the cannibals came for her, dragging her struggling across the wasteland just as they must have dragged her sister. Sometimes they were in the Palace, sometimes in her room. Sometimes they were still there when she woke, screaming.

But tonight, tonight of all nights, she dreamt a different dream. If it was a dream. She knew the tall dark woman who stood by her bedside was Roz Forrester, although how she knew this she did not know. Roz was holding a tray of food - the same tray that Rachellia had brought in. But even as Thandiwe reached out to take some, Roz dashed the tray to the floor. Thandiwe leant out of bed, half out of the thin, torn covers, reaching for the food.

But all she saw was a pile of dry bones, crumbling to dust as she watched. And when she looked up, Roz was gone.

*   *   *

If her mother noticed that Thandiwe stayed thin and gaunt while her courtiers filled out and regained something approaching a healthy glow, she did not comment. Thandiwe did not eat the alien food again after that night, that dream, that visit. But since everyone else ate it, there was sufficient left of the scarce root vegetables they had subsisted on previously for Thandiwe not to go too hungry.

Leabie's mind was on other things. She spent more and more time with Tranlis. He told her something of the Forresters, reading passages from a draft of the history he was preparing. His writing was indeed superior to that of the other historians the former Empress had dealt with, and although he avoided small talk as much as she did, he was pleasant enough company.

After a week, Leabie felt sufficiently at ease to begin to relate her own story. Tranlis listened, asked few questions, took many notes. When Rachellia brought food, Tranlis would often take the opportunity to return to his ship. He told Leabie that he was copying his notes into the ship's storage banks, but she knew he was also eating food from his own supplies.

"Let me take her away, rescue some remnant of your family from this," Tranlis said at one of their sessions.

Leabie looked round, and saw Thandiwe sitting quiet and alone in the shadows at the comer of the room. She was often there, perhaps hoping to remain unnoticed, perhaps not wishing to interrupt. It was good that she was interested in her family. But her place was here on Earth, so Leabie shook her head. "I know your work here is almost done," she replied. "And even with our new-found supplies of food I fear we have little with which we can tempt you to stay when your work is over. Your place is in the stars, relating the great stories of history. And our place, mine and Thandiwe's, is here with our people."

Tranlis leant forward. "But surely the Forresters belong -"

"No." Leabie was firm. "Our place is here. It always has been. You of all people should realize that." A figure stood in the doorway, a welcome distraction. "Ah, Rachellia." Leabie beckoned the woman forward. "Is it time to eat already? When we have been so long between meals, it is difficult to remember what regular mealtimes we should keep."

Rachellia waited by the door. She was wrapped, almost smothered, against the cold. Her eyes were barely visible beneath the hood of her cloak. The ring glinted on her finger as

she folded her hands in front of her, a tiny point of reflected light in the dark folds of the bulky sleeves. It must be colder in the kitchens, Leabie thought. "No doubt you have some tasks that command your attention back at your ship," she said to Tranlis as they stood. "We shall talk again soon."

Leabie held out her hand for Thandiwe. Her daughter took it and helped her to the door. Despite the food, Leabie was getting old and frail. Together they made their way through to the dining hall. "The Palace is quieter than it used to be," Leabie said as they walked. There were few sounds apart from their own footsteps. The dining hall itself was also quiet, a few courtiers standing respectfully at the long table, waiting for their Empress. "I suppose," she said as she took her seat at the head of the table, "that when people have sufficient food, they have less need of leadership."

*   *   *

The three of them sat in the cold. Leabie was exhausted, but her story was nearly finished. Thandiwe sat quiet and still, hands folded on her lap. She was still thin, and her face was drawn but at least she seemed well. Leabie sighed. If only her daughter would eat some of the food, rather than subsisting on what few vegetables Rachellia and the others could find for her. She lacked the healthy glow that the courtiers were acquiring, yet she seemed happy enough. It's her age, Leabie thought; we are lucky that she can afford the luxury of being difficult.

Tranlis was listening attentively as ever. It was as if his whole being was focused on Leabie's story, his life in hers. She had asked him once, early on, what his interests were. He had seemed surprised, and when she pressed him it transpired that he had none. Only his history - her history. For longer than he could remember, he had told her, Tranlis had been obsessed with the past, and the Forrester family was a line traced through history from which he could hang that obsession." He could not remember when he had started his research, his quest. And now that the end of his crusade was in sight, the history almost within his grasp, he had seemed equally uncertain what he would do next.

"I suppose," Leabie had said, "that since our history will continue, so will your work." She had intended it to be a way of closing the subject, of opening another. Tranlis had not answered.

And now it was almost over. He had questions of course, he always had questions. If today, at the finish, they were more insistent, then that was to be expected. Leabie sensed that this was to be their final session. His final audience with the Empress. With that realization came too the pangs of hunger, and Leabie wondered where Rachellia was. They had not eaten for hours. Or was it days?

When they were finished, finally finished, Tranlis offered again, offered to take Thandiwe away from Earth. And again Leabie refused.

"Where is Rachellia?" she demanded. "Go and see what has happened," she told Thandiwe.

*   *   *

The Palace was silent. As Thandiwe made her way to the kitchens, she saw nobody, heard nothing. How long had she sat with her mother and Tranlis, listening to their history? How long had she sat and listened to her mother relate her own story and the stories of her contemporaries? All except Aunt Roz. About her, Leabie had said almost nothing. Yet every night now, Roz was at Thandiwe's bedside, hurling the tray of food to the floor. She stood tall and proud, a contrast to Rachellia's stooped figure, huddled inside the layers of wrappings as she led them each day to eat.

But not today. Today Rachellia was gone. The kitchens were empty, pots and crockery unwashed on the worktops. A large cauldron had boiled dry over a heating element that had burnt out. Dust lay across the floor. They were all gone.

The Palace was empty too. As she went back to the throne room, Thandiwe again saw and heard nobody. The sleeping quarters were deserted, the dining hall empty. A chair lay on its back where it had fallen, as if someone had stood up too quickly. The throne room, she noticed when she returned, was unguarded.

*   *   *

Leabie did not know when she had last been outside the Palace, did not remember. But Tranlis would soon be gone, and she needed to know what was happening. He had offered to bring food from his ship, but his work was done. Better to go with him before he left for good, to see for herself what was abroad in her kingdom, what had called her courtiers and her guards away from the Palace.

She would not take Tranlis's food: He had offered it in payment for her story when he first arrived, but Leabie would rather the story was payment enough itself. When he was gone, she and Thandiwe would still need to eat, and so she had accepted his offer of an escort to the nearest alien ship.

There was food enough there, if Rachellia was to be believed, and Tranlis's weapons would ensure they got there. This time.

It was the brightness that struck her. The Palace, even when the power had been working, was not well lit. It was a place of shadows and half-lights. But outside, the real world was bright with the distant sun. She shielded her eyes and tried to make out the features of the landscape ahead, but there were none. It was exactly as she had imagined, as she had been told. A barren wasteland, a nothing-world, broken and dry. The ruins were worn down so much they barely scratched the sky, their edges blunted and blackened by time. The Divine Empress, her daughter and their escort made their progress through the pale landscape. Their robes, despite age and wear, were splashes of colour against the grey of the ruined Earth. Tranlis had suggested they wear darker clothes, disguise themselves, but Leabie was, when all was said and done, the Empress, and whatever else she might be, or have been, she was proud. And it was her hurt pride more than her relief and surprise that she felt as they passed unremarked through her subjects.

They sat quietly, eyes staring. Their clothes were tom, tattered, but they looked healthy enough. Their faces, when they were not swaddled inside their clothes or hidden in their hands, had the same healthy slightly orange glow that Leabie's courtiers had worn. And they were calm. Every- where there was a disquieting calm, as if now there was no need to scrabble and fight and die for food; as if there was nothing left to be done. Was this how Tranlis would be when his Great Work was complete, when his life was fulfilled and only emp- tiness lay ahead? Leabie stared at the people as she passed, amazed, but they did not return her stare, did not react at all.

Beside her, helping her pick her way through the rubble and the ruin, Thandiwe drew in a sharp breath. "Mother!"

"What is it, my child?"

Thandiwe pointed at a group huddled round a small fire. They were almost entirely wrapped in cloaks. and blankets although it was not too cold. "The cloaks, and the clothes of some of the people we passed earlier. They're the colours of the cannibal gangs. Yet they're just sitting there, quietly."

"We are almost there," Tranlis said before Leabie could answer. "The ship is just beyond the next building."

"You know your way so well," Leabie said quietly. "Is your own ship nearby?"

"My own ship is off to the north, but it maintains a scan of the locations of the other ships." He stopped and turned to face them. "My offer still stands, you know. I can take you and your daughter away from this, back to the stars and glory."

"You know my answer." Leabie gestured to the group huddled round the fire. "These are our people. This is our home."

*   *   *

Leabie had not expected a queue. She was not sure what she had expected, but it was not to wait in a shuffling line of people inching closer to the alien ship. The ship itself was a distorted arrangement of surfaces and edges. It seemed almost crystalline in shape, though it shone like metal. It was more like a building than a vessel, sprung up from the scarred earth. There were hatches along the length of the side nearest them. The line of people curled and stretched past the hatches. And from inside the aliens handed out bowls and boxes of the food.

As they edged closer, the line split so that they were in a shorter queue heading for one of the hatches.

Leabie peered at the dark smudge on the side of the ship, her vision blurred by the sunlight and by age and hunger. She stumbled as her foot struck a broken brick, and Thandiwe caught her.

The alien was reaching out of the hatch, handing the food down to the people below as they pushed past. As they approached, Leabie could begin to see inside, could begin to make out the shape and form of their benefactor. It seemed to be draped in a cloak, not unlike the clothing that the people huddled round the fire had worn, not unlike people in the queue. Not unlike her own courtiers.

But the head that emerged from the rolled-back hood was quite different. It was an orange-skinned dome, smooth but with some features. The features were merely lumps and undulations that caught the sunlight as the creature leant forward. Around the base of the dome was a row of pure white eyes, set into the skin like jewels. They shone and glowed as they swivelled to look down at the next human in the line. At Leabie.

"Take, eat." The voice was soft and female. Hands reached out and down to Leabie, holding a box. There were four hands, emerging from inside the discoloured cloak:. Each hand had three fingers. Leabie reached up to take the box, the sun streaming sideways across the alien's face so that the slight indentations and bumps on the domed head were emphasized, throwing shadows across it.

The face. It looked like a face, just for an instant. As if a face, a human face, were trying to push through the orange skin and break out into the sunlight.

Just for a moment. Then the head moved forward as the alien pushed the box into Leabie's arms and the moment was gone.

Leabie took the box, lifting it gently and gratefully from the hands that held each comer. As she lifted the box away, as she turned to go, she saw the alien hand that had held one of the back comers, saw it as it withdrew into the hatch. On the middle finger was a ring. The hand paused as it retreated. The alien looked down at Leabie and there again was the hint of a face. And in that instant, Leabie recognized two things.

One was the great seal of the Empress, embossed on the face of the courtier's ring. The other was the face so faintly embossed on the domed head.

"Rachellia," she breathed. Then louder: "Rachellia."

Then the man behind her pushed Leabie to one side. She stumbled away as the man reached up for his food. Thandiwe and Tranlis pulled her upright, asked her if she was all right.

But Leabie did not hear them. She was staring first back at the hatch, and then along the line of people queuing in front of it. Was it her imagination, or were the people in the queue taking on a slightly orange hue? Many were wrapped so completely in cloaks and blankets that Leabie could not see their skin. But those whose faces were visible seemed to have features that were slightly flattened, unpronounced. It must be her imagination, but as she looked from face to face Leabie could almost see the noses receding, eyes healing over, mouths closing up, foreheads stretching up into domes. She looked to her daughter for reassurance. But a glance at Thandiwe's face, the features immaculately defined in stark contrast to those of the people in the queue behind her, her complexion pale and fresh by comparison, was enough to confirm Leabie's fears.

Thandiwe had not eaten the food.

*   *   *

She expected Tranlis to tell her she was imagining it, but instead he nodded grimly.

Thandiwe was almost in tears; Leabie felt nothing but numbness and the ache of hunger and loss. Only Tranlis seemed calm and rational. He held up a small device, the same device he had used to make notes during their discussions, a small black cube with rounded corners that fitted into the palm of his hand.

"While you were queuing; I transmitted pictures back to my ship. Had it run an analysis. It found a match."

"So who are they? What do they want from us?" Thandiwe threw her arms out, embracing the wasted world. "What could they possibly want from us? We have nothing left."

91

"They are the Cimliss." The voice was not Tranlis's. It was softer, more precise. It came from the small device he held. It was the voice of his ship. "They are listed as galactic traders."

"Traders?"

"Indeed. They use bioengineered products to corner the market in various goods and items around the fringes of the "galaxy. However, they are not known for their compassion and there have been disquieting rumours about their business practices. It seems their little empire is expanding, and a lot of races who used to deal with them have just... vanished."

They were walking now. Without comment but by mutual agreement they were making their way towards Tranlis's ship. As they walked, the people queuing behind them stepped ever closer to the food they needed. Stepped ever closer to their fate. And as they walked, the ship continued to talk to them.

"It is rumoured the Cimliss are acquiring planets that have fallen to their lowest point on the basis that at least some of them will increase in value in the longer term. Earth, for instance, may be broken and irrelevant to the galaxy now, but it may be on a vital trade and commerce route in a thousand years, and then the Cimliss will control it."

"An invasion," Leabie marvelled softly, almost pleased that someone was still interested in the planet. "Who would have thought it?"

"They do not invade in the conventional sense,"

the ship admonished. "They do not use weapons, they do not fight. They work from within, turning the populations of the planets they want into themselves and taking the planet by stealth."

In front of them the ship was visible on the horizon. But it was to the box in Tranlis's hand that Leabie turned. She waved away Thandiwe's help, and pulled herself upright. "By stealth or by weapons, they will not invade Earth while I am her Empress."

Thandiwe took her arm again. "But mother - "

"What can you do?" Tranlis asked at the same moment.

She looked at them both. "There will be others," she said. "Others who are still fit and well. Still human. Just as we are. Some will not yet have succumbed, others - like you, Thandiwe - will not have eaten their food, or not enough of it." She felt invigorated, enlivened, young again as she looked into her daughter's eyes. "Don't you see, Thandiwe? My people need me more now than ever." Somewhere in the background, perhaps only in her mind, she could feel an expectant hush into which her words rang out. "We shall fight the invaders to the last breath of humanity and drive them from our planet! My people need me! My people depend on me!"

*   *   *

They stood at the door of the ship. Thandiwe was

surprised at the change in her mother. Just an hour ago she had seemed old and broken. Now she was invigorated, purposeful. She had spoken almost without pause on their journey, outlining her plans for mustering an army and organizing resistance. She had spoken of the hardship that would follow, of how it would be nothing compared to the purposeless starvation they had faced previously. She had spoken of how humanity would triumph, how humanity always triumphed.

And now they stood outside Tranlis's ship with the sun setting on the distant horizon. An end and a beginning. Thandiwe was not surprised at her mother's request, she had half expected it. Tranlis had not reiterated his oft-made offer, but probably he knew he did not have to.

The rationalization, the excuse, was that Thandiwe would be gathering support, raising funds and acquiring equipment. But they all knew that this had failed before. When the Earth lay starving, nobody had heeded the calls for help and supply. Why should they be any more bothered now? Perhaps Leabie really did think that Thandiwe could succeed where her other ambassadors had failed, that there would be more support or a military cause than for a humanitarian one. But if she was right on that score, then perhaps humanity was best left to die in peace.

They said their good-byes. Tranlis left them together, excused himself to see to his ship. Mother and daughter embraced together for the last time on a dying planet beneath a setting sun. Their tears mingled on their touching cheeks as they both struggled for the words and sentiments they felt but could not articulate. In the end they said nothing, and it was more meaningful and sad than any vocabulary could bear.

Thandiwe looked back as she stepped inside the ship. For a precious moment the figure in front of her was upright and young, like the woman at the bedside of her dreams. Then the moment evaporated and Thandiwe's mother smiled weakly at her. An old woman standing alone at the end of the world. The setting sun gave her shadowed face an orange tinge where the light met the dark.

Then the shadows lengthened as the old woman turned away. Thandiwe watched as the Divine Empress, once Glory of the Empire, previous Ruler of the High Court, prior Lord of the Inner and Outer Worlds, quondam High Admiral of the Galactic Fleets, former Lord General of the Six Armies and past Defender of the Earth, Leabie Inyathi Forrester, walked towards the failing sunset.

*   *   *

The Earth was a fading ball of grey and brown, receding behind them. Once, Thandiwe had read, it had been blue and green, with the white of clouds wreathed about it, but now there was just the polluted oceans and the rubble of the cities. The clouds were gone, and no rain fell. An old lady at the end of her life, clinging desperately and in vain to past glories.

"What chance has she got?" Thandiwe asked. 'She is a determined woman."

Tranlis had assumed she was speaking of her mother, and perhaps she was. Asking for reassurance, for lies. But she got none.

She has been eating the infected food for too long, I fear. The poison is already working in her system. Determination will not, I think, be sufficient to overcome it."

The ship added its diagnosis, the words filtered through to Thandiwe as she looked at the image on the virtual screen and silently wept. "The Cimliss virus will already be altering her body. She is not a Forrester any longer, she is something else, something in transition."

'So it is finished." Thandiwe let out a long breath and turned to face Tranlis.

Tranlis nodded. 'Soon," he said. 'very soon now, it will all be over." Then he smiled. "And I shall be free of my task." He looked over Thandiwe's shoulder at the virtual representation of Earth, looked past and through her as if she were no longer there. "The final chapter is almost written. The end of the Forresters."

"No." Her voice was hardly more than a whimper. "What about me? For as long as I am alive, so are the Forresters. So is our family and its history and tradition. You can't close the book while I still live." She had meant to sound defiant, meant for this to be the start of her authority, her reign. But it was more like the dying cadences of an aria.

"While you still live." The echo was the ship as it repeated her words. As it spoke the world slowed, paused, froze. She saw Tranlis turn towards her, a slow motion of the head as it swivelled. A slow curl of the mouth as the smile rippled up and across his face.

In the moment he turned Thandiwe saw him listening so intently to Leabie, heard him ask again and again to take Thandiwe with him, saw him smile and smile. Saw Roz Forrester standing behind him in the shadows, at the front of an endless line of dark-skinned men and women, each with right hand on the shoulder of the one in front, the meagre illumination highlighting their sharp cheekbones and the strong lines of their jaws. Each of them was wearing different clothes from the others, but each was somehow staring at Tranlis through the same pair of eyes. Accusing. Angry.

And she knew.

When Tranlis came at her, she was ready for him. In that moment of action she had a lifetime to prepare herself. His hands reacted for her throat, and she smashed them away. She had a strength, a vigour, she had not experienced before. He hit at her again, but she parried his blow. She grabbed for the nearest thing to use as a defence. It fitted neatly into her hand, felt like a part of her. It was polished wood. priceless. A long club resting on a display stand amid the technology of the flight deck. She grabbed it, lifted it down, continued the action into a full swing.

The club connected with Tranlis's temple and he stopped dead. The smile was still on his face, frozen. A trickle of blood ran down the side of his dented head, the only movement at the still point of the world. Then Tranlis sat down heavily on the floor, his head fell forwards, and he toppled on to his side. The smile was still embossed on his face, the blood pooling round it.

The shadows at the back of the room deepened, and the figures who stood and watched faded into the blackness. But as she went, Thandiwe thought that Roz Forrester smiled. Then there was nothing.

Or almost nothing: a faint glow, a glimmer in the dark.

Thandiwe stepped towards the shadows, the club falling to her feet, spinning to rest on the cold floor. She peered into the darkness, wiping a single tear from her eye. Somewhere at the back of the shadows a metallic shape floated on a virtual screen. Its segmented body was almost foetal as it turned to face her, the light from its glowing eyes glinting on the skin and throwing patterns on the wall.

"Who - what are you?"

"I am the ship." The shape twisted in the darkness. "Your flagship, Empress."

Thandiwe smiled. "You're not much of an imperial fleet."

The form faded away, was gone. Perhaps like the other shadow-shapes it had never been there at all.

"Your family has done more with less before now," the ship said. "You can now write your own history. Your own story."

Thandiwe nodded. "Yes," she said. "That's true." She blinked away her tears, heard the slight break in her voice. "We built an empire. And now we must rebuild it."

As the Earth faded from the screen, Thandiwe Forrester thought she could hear singing in the darkness outside. Or crying.

BLOOD ON THE TRACKS

I remember a time when there was a tribe of hundreds of people living around the Circle. Now there are only Rober, Marger, Philo and me.

With nothing else to do all day but hide from the Vethkin, I find that I spend a lot of time in the past. I can spend hours reconstructing a particular moment from my time back on Earth: the way the light fell on the hair of my mother; the feel of the clothes I was wearing; the weight of my new-born daughter in my arms. Other memories force themselves on me no matter how I try to avoid them: such as the way my ship fell, clumsy and powerless, into one of this planet's oceans, and the way I had to swim to safety on the shore as it sank. And yet, more and more, it is the memory of food that I find myself drawn to, food like I had never encountered before crashing here. I remember the sharp, smoky taste of chicken, blackened on a trader's coals and dipped in spice. I remember juice so tart that it made my eyes water, and beer sweet with honey and black with malt. I remember lamb rolled in rosemary and cooked slowly so that the meat fell from the bone under its own weight, trailing slow, glutinous strings of fat behind it.

Amazing how things that were once beneath my notice now consume my thoughts.

Amazing how many hours I can spend recalling the spikiness of a pineapple, the reptilian markings on a watermelon's skin. That's all the past is now for me: a long table of rough wood, bowed beneath the weight of a banquet; a memory of plenty in a time of famine.

You'll have to forgive me: I have had a lot of time on my hands recently. Time in which I have become caught in the whirring wheels of my own thoughts. Crouched in the dark. Listening to Marger murmuring to herself, and the high, sad sound of the Vethkin. And yet whatever I start out thinking about, whatever philosophical considerations preoccupy my thoughts, I end up dreaming of food.

Marger talks to herself in a low, wheedling voice from the moment she wakes up until the moment she falls asleep. Philo doesn't say anything at all: his legs were burned away during the cull and he spends his waking hours staring at the small scraps of blue sky visible through the thorn bushes, absently scratching at itches where his knees once were. Only Rober and I are left, one of us always out scavenging amongst the ruins and the grasslands for food while the other replaces the concealing bushes when the wind whips them away from our refuge, and tries to stop Marger from talking too loudly when the Vethkin appear in the sky.

More often than not, it is Rober who goes scavenging. He was a farmer, and knows the ways of the land. More importantly, perhaps, he cannot stand hearing Marger talk, so he doesn't mind spending most of his time away from the refuge. She was his wife, before the cull, but now - now I clean her, and feed her, and listen to her endless, meaningless jabber. There is precious little else I can do. I was once a pilot, then, after I crashed on this world and was accepted by its human inhabitants — a lost and debased tribal remnant of Earth's previous colonial migrations I became its historian and storyteller, and the few times Rober stayed behind and I went out I ended up returning either empty-handed or, on one occasion, with a cluster of berries that Rober just looked at with disdain.

"Poisonous," he said curtly.

"How do you know?"

"l just know." And he turned to leave the refuge, looking for food we could eat.

They didn't look poisonous. They looked full to bursting, and dusky skinned. Rober threw them out of the refuge with an angry flick of his hand, and all I could do for the next hour or more was sit and watch the birds peck at them, scattering juice and gobbets of flesh.

We tried catching the birds, but they are wary of us and their meat is rank and dry. Not that we would let that stop us - not now, not with the hunger perpetually squirming in our distended stomachs – but whenever we succeeded in trapping a bird older or more stupid than the rest we spent the next day doubled up with cramps. Perhaps because they do eat the berries. There was a poem I remember reading, as a child back on Earth, a poem about a seafarer who found himself drifting, abandoned, dying of thirst while surrounded by water too salty to drink. That's the way I feel as I watch birds we cannot eat fight over berries we cannot eat.

Sometimes we eat well and sometimes we eat badly, but Rober usually manages to bring something back for us. A rabbit-like animal, caught in one of his many snares. A wild thing like a piglet, brought down with a well-aimed stone. An Alsatian — descended from pets brought by the original colonists, I assume — once kept us going for a whole week, which was about the time it took the bite marks to heal. Rober strangled it one-handed while its jaws were clamped around his forearm. Or so he told me.

The way he looks at his wife sometimes, I think he would like to do the same to her.

I try to leave the refuge for a while, every day, just to get some time to myself. Just to see the clouds cruising calmly across the sky like huge and distant spacecraft. I can hear the Vethkin long before I can see them, or they can see me. I always have time to hurry back to the refuge — just one of many clumps of thorny bushes sprouting randomly across the grasslands — before they appear.

It's obvious to me that the Vethkin are some form of alien race. Perhaps they are the original inhabitants of this planet, or perhaps they use it as a transit stop on their way to somewhere else, but to the tribe — who had lost all knowledge of other worlds, other races — they were a supernatural phenomenon. They appear in the sky like huge, metallic fruit, heralded by a sound like a thin, lonely trumpet, then vanish suddenly only to appear again a few hundred metres away, progressing in a series of hops and skips against the blue backdrop. Perhaps they are spacecraft, perhaps they are the Vethkin themselves. I don't know. All the tribe ever saw were the objects themselves. until the events leading up to the cull.

I think it was the Vethkin who caused me to crash. I don't believe it was intentional, but I have a fuzzy recollection of my ship being suddenly surrounded by brightly coloured objects - other spacecraft, I thought at the time — then losing all power and tumbling from orbit. I remember my vision twisting as the ship fell, as though the three dimensions of its construction - possibly even time as well — were being warped. And then I remember nothing apart from the water, the waves and the fight to get to the shore. It is difficult to tell from the fragmentary records and oral traditions of the tribe whether the Vethkin were there when the colonists arrived or whether they appeared some time later. I suspect that the Vethkin are somehow tied into the decay of what must once have been a thriving Earth colony into a tribe that had lost all knowledge of their origins on another world, but that is speculation on my part. Whatever the truth, the Vethkin had been part of the background of the colonists' lives for so long that the children had made them into part of their games.

There is a circle made of some substance like stone only smoother and warmer, near to where the tribe lived, and the objects appear and disappear inside it. It was not part of the ruins, for it was made o/a material that could not be scratched or cut, and the tribe just called it the Circle. It was so obvious, so much a part of their daily lives, that they didn't even think about it.

After long and careful observation — the kind that only children can make - the tribe worked out that an object would appear in the sky for a few seconds before disappearing again. If it didn't reappear instantly elsewhere in the sky then they knew that it would reappear in the Circle itself. There it would stay for a few moments, suspended a few inches above the ground and singing gently to itself, before vanishing again and appearing back in the sky, some distance from where they had been before. Sometimes another one would replace the vanished one straight away; sometimes it was almost a minute before the Circle was occupied again. They could never be sure.

The children used to gather by the lip of the stone, some ten or eleven of them. Lots would be drawn by some arcane process, and one of them chosen. The chosen one would stand on the grass, just outside the Circle, and run across to the other side. If they made it before one of the objects appeared in the Circle, they won. If not... Well, that never happened. The trick, or so one child told me, was to fix on particular patterns and shapes: an orange and green checkerboard sphere, perhaps, or a series of swirls on a ribbed ovoid. That particular object would disappear from the sky as they watched, and then it would be in the Circle. They knew that although there was no fixed interval between the disappearance of one object from the Circle and the appearance of the next, they could count rapidly to ten between the disappearance of an object from the sky and its appearance in the Circle. For the duration of that count, no other object could appear.

Could - or would? They didn't know, and they didn't care. It was one of the laws of their world, like rain following dark clouds, or an abundance of food following a harvest. They were kids, playing games. Running across the warm stone, lungs burning, legs on fire. There were stories about those who had failed in the past — the objects had appeared around them and carried them away, or had squashed them like fruit jam, or had left them intact but changed in a way that meant they were taken away by their families and never talked of again - but none of them had even seen these things, only heard about them in hushed, serious tones, and I could never track the stories down to actual facts. Legends, that's all they were. I'm sure children always told macabre stories like that. Even before the Vethkin came.

The children of the tribe assumed that the objects were unaware of them, in the way that trees, and clouds, and houses were unaware. They also assumed that they were the only ones who had realised about the count of ten between them disappearing from the sky and appearing in the Circle.

Not that they knew about such concepts as exclusivity, or fixed times. They just knew if they did this then the result was this. The mathematical logic behind it did not interest them.

In fact, in my assumed role as historian to the tribe, I realised that such knowledge was known to all the elders. It was not spoken of not because it was secret, but because it was trivial. Uninteresting. The objects did what the objects did — appeared, disappeared, appeared, disappeared. The tribe did what they did — grew food, herded animals, had festivals and traded with other tribes. There was no connection.

It seems like years ago that things changed, but it can only be a few months. A harsh winter had given way to a blazing hot summer, and neither of them had done the crops any good. The tribe weren't starving, but there was an ever-present worry over where the next week's food was coming from. Even the fish didn't seem to be biting in the lake. Many times I had been asked by the elders whether there were any precedents in the records, and I had to answer fairly that there were, but not many. As my own stipend — food and shelter, provided as a tithe on the tribe as a whole — depended on the elders, I couldn't help but wonder if I shouldn't be telling them something more helpful.

I was sitting cross-legged on top of a hill that overlooked the tents and rough huts that constituted the village, running through the list of village Elders who had lived and died since... well, since someone first started keeping a list; their names, what rulings they passed, what notable judgements they made, whether they were considered good or bad. There were several hundred names, but it was important to get the list right because there were other lists - the laws of the tribe, the rules that told of who could marry whom, the precepts for greeting emissaries from other - that hung off the list of Elders. Like fruit from a bush. Like ripe, dusky fruit. From where I sat I could see the Circle: a grey stain on the landscape. Young kids were gathered around its edge, playing the games that other children had played before them. Watching. Waiting. Counting. Then running, running as fast as they could across the smooth, grey surface. A girl reached the edge of the Circle, pony-tail streaming behind her, fists clenched in triumph, and I remember thinking that my own daughter, who I had left behind so many years ago, would be about her age. As the sadness welled up within me, I saw a rippling of the air as one of the Vethkin's strange objects pushed its way into existence in the centre, erupting from the air like a duck surfacing in a lake. It hovered there, a foot or so above the ground, about twice the height o/a man and three times as wide. Its orange skin was furrowed from top to bottom, and it had a greenish patina like old copper.

The kids linked hands in a circle around the Circle, chanting some rhyme I didn't know. They dropped hands and bent down, picking stones and twigs from the ground. Straightening, they threw their miniature collection of weapons at the object. They bounced off its hard surface with bell-like chimes that I could just make out from my position on the hill. It sat there for a few moments longer, paying no attention to them, basking in the afternoon sun, and then it sank into the air and was gone.

I scanned the sky, waiting for its reappearance. There seemed to be more of the objects around than I remembered. For a while there was nothing, and then I saw it appear against the deep blue, hovering over the edges of the village. And then it was gone again, off on its way to who knew where?

The kids reformed into a small knot on one side of the Circle, daring one of their number to make the run. I couldn't tell from that range who it was, although I could see the tension in his stance.

One of the girls in the ground reached out and touched his hand. I think

he smiled.

Like him, I let my eyes flicker amongst the many alien shapes in the sky, waiting for one to disappear. Once it did, he had a count of ten to run from one side of the Circle to the other. A count of ten. It sounds like an age, but when your heart is pumping, when the bitter metal taste of fear is in your mouth, when your legs feel too weak to carry your weight, it is less than a heartbeat.

A shape seemed to ripple and vanish somewhere

over the corn fields. It was yellow stippled with green, and spiked.

Just as I was about to turn back and watch him run, something caught my attention. Another shape, a lumpy mass of purple dark against the white of the clouds, vanished as I watched.

That couldn't have happened. I must have been mistaken. During the whole of my time stranded on the planet, the rules of the game had never changed. The objects hung in the sky. Eventually one would vanish. Moments later it would appear in the circle. Then it would vanish again and appear in the sky. I had never seen two vanish at the same time. Nobody had. In all the stories, in all the histories I had memorised, there was no mention of this.

One or two of the kids had noticed, down around the Circle. The one who was preparing to run was already off, oblivious to anything else: legs pumping, arms flailing, eyes screwed shut. The girl who had touched his hand was trying to call him back, but even if he had heard her it was too late. He reached the far side of the Circle with his arms aloft in triumph, and as he crossed the lip the first of the objects appeared in the centre, swimming out of the air.

And then so did the second.

The two objects intersected. Green and yellow spikes erupted through rents in purple skin. A high-pitched keening cut through the air, turning heads in the village and across the fields. The children scattered as the two shapes appeared to burst open, each exploding the other. Enmeshed, they hit the Circle with a sound like the tolling of a huge, cracked bell and listed to one side. Something fleshy fell from them in long gobbets and lay, Wet and stark, on the grey material of the Circle.

For a moment the world seemed suspended, and then everyone seemed to be moving at once. The children were running away from the Circle as last as the adults were running toward it, pouring out of the village, the fields and the woods, abandoning their back-breaking attempts to tend the straggly crops and the thin animals. I scrambled down the hill side as fast as I could. This was a story that would be told for hundreds of generations. I had to be there. I had to see it all.

I arrived with the first of the villagers, and as they edged closer I stood and watched what they did as much as what had happened. The first thing that struck me was the smell: sharp and yet curiously sweet. Raspberry vinegar, I thought.

The ruins of the two Vethkin objects were spread over most of the surface of the Circle. It was as if someone had smashed two huge watermelons Into one another. Fragments of what had to be a shell an inch thick projected from a mass of pulpy grey material; something like curds, only firmer.

And then the pulpy material twitched.

I wasn't the first to spot it. One of the tribal elders who was bending over, prodding the stuff with a stick, suddenly sprang back with an oath.

"It's moving!" he cried.

After that, everyone wanted to poke at it. I edged closer, fascinated by the way the grey stuff inflated and deflated slightly, as if in time to some distant pulse, and would flinch away if touched. People were leaning in and retrieving fragments of shell as souvenirs. The sense of shock and cosmic catastrophe that had initially spread over everyone gradually but surely turned into a party atmosphere.

In the rush to pick over the remains of whatever had happened — the most extraordinary thing to occur to the tribe within living memory - everyone had forgotten what the Circle was for. What happened in it. As the realisation struck me I took several steps toward the lip and glanced upward.

The sky was empty. Devoid of the Vethkin objects. Another first.

I gazed at the villagers, scrabbling amongst the ruins of something mysterious, something that they had always taken for granted and yet never understood, and I was struck by an almost hysterical sense of… inappropriateness. They should have been solemn. They should have been reverent. Instead they were acting like farmers' wives at market day.

I say "they" as if I was separate from them, but by that time I was as much part of the tribe as anyone else, despite my origins elsewhere, despite my wife and daughter back on Earth.

It was when I saw one of the local dogs sniff cautiously at the grey curds that I had my first presentiment of disaster. I took a step towards it, hoping to shoo it away, but before I could do anything the scrawny mutt cautiously licked a clump of the stuff, not put off by the sharp smell. Wagged its tail. Looked around to see whether it was doing anything wrong. And then took a great bite. Before it could even swallow the first mouthful, it was snuffling up a second.

One of the villagers, a carpenter by the name of Jonat, was watching the dog. He'd been hit particularly hard by short food supplies: he had five young children and an invalid wife, and as he wasn't a farmer he had to barter his services for grain and then find the time to grind it into flour. His cheeks were hollowed through hard work and malnutrition, and his hungry gaze was locked on the dog's increasingly frantic feeding.

"Master," he said to a passing elder, "is this... can we... can we eat it?"

The elder looked over at me. I shrugged: we were in fresh waters now. He looked at the dog, which seemed to be suffering no ill effects. Its muzzle was coated in the grey curds now, and it was licking itself happily.

"Perhaps this is the answer to our prayers," he said slowly. "Perhaps God has seen fit to provide food for Her starving children. Collect it up. Fetch buckets and store it in the cool-houses before the sun dries it out. And catch that dog: if nothing has happened to it by tomorrow morning then we will see." He nodded sagely. "Yes, we will see."

I wanted to protest, but I had no grounds. There was a phrase used back on Earth that had also passed into the tribe's vocabulary, but without any meaning attached - manna from heaven - but that hardly gave me any grounds for objecting. Perhaps he was right; perhaps it was a gift from God.

I glanced again at the empty sky. Something was wrong, but the old stories didn't tell me what it was, and there were no clues in what was happening now.

I stayed for a few hours in the blazing sun, watching the tribe collect the grey stuff up into whatever containers they could find and carry it back to the village. By the time they had finished, all that was left of the two Vethkin objects was a collection of shell fragments covered in grey slime; and the smell, so sharp at the beginning, had mellowed to the mellow fruitiness of a good red wine.

I saw Jonat licking his fingers as he piled great gobbets of the stuff into an old watering can. Others slipped bits into their mouths when they thought nobody was watching. No immediate harm seemed to come to them.

And the sky was empty all the time they worked.

I stayed there, as the sun slipped slowly down towards the horizon. The crowd thinned until there were only a few sightseers left. The kids who had been playing there originally returned, amazed that their playground was now the focus of so much activity. By sunset I was the only one still there.

I sat, waiting, a few feet away from the Circle, as the sky darkened into night, as the birds quietened down and as night creatures began to forage in the shadows around me. Firelight from the village illuminated the sky, and I could hear sounds o/a party. I was waiting for something, but I wasn't sure what.

I think I slid into sleep at one stage. I remember confused dreams of fire, and screaming, and o/ me climbing through piles of rubble looking for someone whose face I had forgotten.

And when I awoke, one of the Vethkin objects was hovering in the centre of the Circle.

It was the largest object I had ever seen; smooth and black, with a faint blue ripple shifting across its skin. Beams of light played beneath it, illuminating the broken shards of the other objects. It hung there for what must have been an hour. I watched it, entranced. Whether it knew I was there or not I don't know, but eventually the beams of light vanished and the object submerged into the air, taking the shards and the scummy remnants of the grey material with it.

Automatically I lifted my eyes to the sky, and felt my throat constrict around my breath.

There were hundreds of red objects hanging like needles from the low, dark clouds. They were positioned over the village, and as I watched they flexed, drawing their ends together and increasing their diameter. They held that posture for a few moments, and then relaxed, and as they relaxed the quality of the night changed. I don't know if it got quieter, or if the wind suddenly dropped, or what, but something changed. Something changed forever.

The objects all vanished from the sky at the same time, and my eyes registered a flicker in the middle of the circle as if they all passed through it within the space o/a few heartbeats. Or in the time it might take me to count to ten.

When the sky and the circle were both empty, I ran to the village.

Where everyone was dead. The houses stood as they had always stood, the animals milled around in confusion, looking to me for guidance as I ran past them, screaming, but the people were dead. Most were in their beds, for it was well after sunset. Some were slumped over tables in the tavern or had fallen where they stood in the street.

I found Marger in a root cellar. Whatever strange influence the Vethkin had exerted over the town had failed to penetrate the ground enough to kill her, although it had certainly turned her mind. Philo I found in his baker's shop. I never knew what saved him, but he, appeared to have lost consciousness and slipped into his own fire. His legs were ruined below the knee. Rober had been out in the fields. He never told me why. He was the one who cut the wreckage of Philo's legs away.

We survive, the four of us. We eat — sometimes. We drink — most of the time. We avoid the gaze of the Vethkin, as they appear and disappear in the sky. We don't talk much, but we all remember. Even Marger.

Rober thinks the Vethkin are looking for us. He believes they intend finishing off the few survivors of their cull.

I am not so sure.

It happened the last time I went out by myself, looking for food. I knew of a small pool near the Circle, an offshoot of a tributary that feeds into the lake, where fish tend to congregate. I used to swim there, before the cull. It was shortly after sunrise, and the shadows were long on the ground. I scurried along, bent almost double, ready to fling myself beneath a bush if I heard the lonely solo trumpet that heralded the appearance of a Vethkin object in the sky.

I don't know why I didn't hear it. Perhaps it was too far away. Perhaps the Vethkin had redesigned the objects since the cull. Or perhaps I just didn't want to hear it. Whatever the reason, I was crossing the edge of the Circle, on my way to the pool, when the object appeared. Taller than I was, shaped like a pear and coloured in bright streaks of orange and violet.

There was nowhere to hide. I was less than six feet away from it. Somewhere far away I could hear a sound, as if a brass band were playing out of tune.

I stared at the object. The object just sat there, playing its sad music.

"You bastards!" I screamed, shocking myself. "You killed them. You killed them all!"

The object didn't react.

I took a step towards it, not sure what I intended to do, but it slowly faded from sight as if more and more of the landscape were coming between me and it. And then it was gone.

"You bastards," I whispered. "You just don't care."

After a while I wandered back to the refuge. Rober asked about the fish, but I told him they weren't biting that day.

I never told Rober about encountering the object. If we didn't have the comfort of the shelter, if we didn't have the constant threat of the Vethkin, what would we have? What would we do?

And now, every day, when I know that Rober is off hunting for food, I walk up to the Circle, and I wait. I wait for a Vethkin object to appear in the sky, and when it does I wait for it to disappear. If it reappears instantly somewhere else in the sky, I do nothing. If it doesn't reappear, I start running. Running and counting.

Our diet isn't too good, despite Rober's best efforts, and I'm not getting any younger. One day I'm not going to make it in time.

Or perhaps, one day, I might just stop halfway.

Just to see if the stories the children used to tell one another are true.

A FLEETING GLIMPSE

The shelves of the Great Library at Ghazar climb upward, like geometrical cliffs, to touch the distant ceiling. Halfway up, the various books, scrolls, data crystals and other, more exotic forms of information storage reverse themselves, stacked upside down so that the Ghazarite scholars who scuttle across the ceiling can access them easily.

It occurred to Katie Forrester, as she watched one scholar remove a dusty bundle of scent-globes from a niche, that it was a particularly overt form of academic oppression. The Ghazarites could access the archives from both directions - the ground and the ceiling. Visitors from other planets were restricted to just half the collection, unless they either hired a local researcher - expensive, and critically dependent on how meticulous the researcher was suspended themselves precariously from the forest of hooks that previous visitors had left screwed into the ceiling and tried to read the titles on the various items upside down, or climbed the stacks using ropes and pitons.

Or, like Katie, use electro-binoculars and a trained Noort.

The electro-binoculars enabled her to see even the titles on the very top shelf, right next to the ceiling. Basic image-processing software corrected for the viewing angle and flipped the picture so that the titles were oriented the right way, while a visual translator overlaid them with a good approximation of their English equivalent. The Noort had an amazingly extendible and very sticky tongue, and would follow simple orders in exchange for cinnamon-iced biscuits. Orders such as "Fetch!", accompanied by Katie pointing towards whichever item she wanted.

The electro-binoculars and the Noort had seemed like a good idea five days earlier when Katie had started searching through the archive. Now all she had was a headache, eyestrain, and sticky fingers from the residue left by the Noort's tongue.

And none of them were what she was looking for.

Aggravated, she reached out to intercept a passing Ghazarite researcher. The Ghazarites were identical to the eyes of most visitors - bundles of walking sticks tied together with dirty twine and covered with cobwebs — but the researchers were easily distinguishable thanks to the crimson rings around each of their dusty, bamboo-like limbs and the meters hanging from a strap around their middle.

"I need assistance," she said.

The Ghazarite pressed a button on its meter, which started ticking loudly, counting off credits with frightening rapidity. It said nothing, watching her with eyes like bunches of grapes.

"I'm looking for a record," she continued. "It's a personal narrative, written in ink on paper by a human being who crashed on an unnamed planet and lived for some years with the natives. It's about thirty years old. It was bequeathed to the Library by a collector of Earth antiquities and curios about ten years ago." She gestured towards the ceiling. "It should be up there. You can see the gap."

The Ghazarite's attention switched to where Katie was pointing, although she wasn't sure how she could tell. "Sociology, Mutters Spiral, Earth," it whispered. "That particular record is on extended loan to a Jullati historian."

"This is a research library, not a lending library," Katie shouted. Heads and cobwebby limbs around the room turned towards her.

"It is a lending library if the price is right, and that particular record is of no intrinsic value," the Ghazarite said. "It duplicates information we already have and provides no new insight into human social interactions. And speaking of price..."

Suppressing a curse, Katie rooted around in her pockets for some loose change. "You're not getting a red cent until I get the name of that historian," she muttered.

*   *   *

Katie had assumed that the Jullati historian who had borrowed the record from the Great Library of Ghazar was actually working on Ghazar. In fact, he (or she, or it — Katie didn't know a great deal about Jullati biology) had returned to Jullat with the journal. And Katie had followed, leaving her Noort regretfully behind with a big pile of cinnamon-iced biscuits.

Jullat was a dried-up prune of a world, old and scarred by conflict and by ecological catastrophe. Low cities covered the surface, built on top of, around and beneath each other with a tired carelessness, as if the Jullati no longer cared about how their planet looked to visitors. And judging by the number of handbooks and rulebooks that were consulted by puzzled Jullati customs officials when Katie landed, they didn't get very many visitors.

She found the historian in an irregularly octagonal office in one of the planet's many universities. The floor was covered by archival records of many different types, from scent globes to data crystals, from dead memory turtles to massive leather-bound volumes. He — or she, or it — was elephantine and wrinkled, and looked as old and as tired as its planet. "I apologise for disturbing you," she began, "but I am trying to find a record that you borrowed from the Great Library of Ghazar. It's a journal, written by a human male on a planet with no name. I... I need to consult that record."

"Ah," the Jullati wheezed. It seemed to sink into reminiscence. "Ahhh..." it said again.

"The record?"

"Ahhhh..."

She waited for the historian to continue, but it just stood there on its eight massive legs, filling the office and breathing heavily. She was just about to say something else when it spoke again.

"I have been writing a dissertation on the history of the Vethkin for many centuries. You are familiar with the Vethkin?"

She racked her memory. She had a good working knowledge of most races, living or dead, but the Vethkin had escaped her.

"I don't think so," she said cautiously.

"They exist only partly in this dimension, and their home planet, if they have one, is not contiguous with our reality. They have been glimpsed, appearing and disappearing, on many planets, and at certain locations in free space. I have been attempting to assemble everything known about them into a coherent narrative history. It is proving... difficult."

Many centuries, Katie thought. Yes, that suggested it was hard.

"And the record?" she asked.

"I noted what it said about the Vethkin, and I passed it on to a Karnite colleague, having made sure I properly referenced it in my dissertation, of course." The Jullati's skin rippled. "There was little I did not already know about the Vethkin."

She bit her tongue to stop herself from swearing. "And what about the human who wrote the journal? Did he have a name?"

The Jullati shrugged; a massive movement of its entire body. "Not my field," it said. "I did not make any notes about the human."

If it hadn't been five times her body mass, Katie would have punched the alien. "Can you tell me the name of your colleague?" she asked. "Where can I find it?"

"On a sightseeing tour of the Greater Magellanic Cloud," the Jullat said. "It will be back in a century or two..."

*   *   *

It took Katie Forrester three weeks to find the cruise liner *Arboline Queen*. Most of that time she spent in a stasis field in her small but luxuriously equipped spacecraft. After all, why use up a small but noticeable fraction of her lifespan cooped up in a tin can, obsessing about the object of her search, when she could be frozen in time? The ship was equipped with state-of-the art entertainment and learning facilities, but they were just a way of distracting her attention from the inevitable ticking away of her life.

She found the *Arboline Queen* stationary in space near one the Magellanic Cloud's rarest sights: a planet poised, like a fly in amber, between the gravity wells of three stars in a trinary system. The slightest perturbation in any direction would result in the planet slowly but surely falling into the gravity well of one of the stars, The inhabitants - a pre-spacefaring race of moderate intelligence — were paranoid about earthquakes, atomic bombs and meteor strikes. Many of them were cooperating in a desperate attempt to develop space-flight before it was too late. The rest were trying to stop them, on the basis that even a handful of rocket launches from the same spot could cause the planet to shift slightly, putting it on the path to disaster. And all the time, ships from various alien races hung out in the infinite blackness of space; watching, analysing, enjoying.

"It's blissfully tragic," said the Karnite historian that Katie had contacted. It was difficult to tell scale from the snowflake-like image on the screen, but she somehow got the impression that the Karnite was small. Possibly very small. "I do so love species on the verge of extinction. They have a desperate vitality about them that is quite breath-taking. Some of the most affecting art in the galaxy comes from species who are no longer with us."

"Like the Vethkin?" Katie hazarded.

The Karnite shuddered: ripples along its many arms making it chime gently. "Nobody knows whether the Vethkin are extinct or not, although they haven't been seen for some time now. And what little Vethkin art survives is five- or six-dimensional. Several critics and collectors have been driven mad just looking at it."

"But you have been researching the Vethkin?" Katie pressed. "You took a manuscript of an encounter with the Vethkin from a researcher on Jullat."

"Yes, but not because of the Vethkin," the

historian protested. "I was more interested in the inhabitants of the planet mentioned in the narrative — driven to the brink of extinction by the ruthless predation of a superior alien race. I wanted to discover more about how they coped with those final days. How they came to terms with the inevitability of their demise."

"And did you?"

"No." More chimes, as the Karnite shivered. "According to the narrative, they were not an indigenous species, just a lost colony of some other race. They had no history to lose, no civilisation of their own to die; just the tattered remnants of some forgotten progenitor."

"And the manuscript?" Katie asked, trying to keep the emotion from her voice.

"I do not have it."

"What are the odds?" Katie muttered. "What did you do with it?"

"I sold it to a colleague on this vessel: a Rebeekan. He was intrigued by the crude and yet aesthetic nature of some sketches and diagrams made in the margins of the material that the narrative was written on."

She took a deep breath to mask her rising frustration. "Could I speak to this colleague?"

"Sadly, no. It left the ship at our last port of call. Apparently, there was some kind of catastrophe back on its home world." There were several million kilometres of clear vacuum between Katie's ship and the precariously poised world, but Katie's swearing was so loud that observers on the *Arboline Queen* were worried that it might disturb the planet's orbit and send it plunging into one or other of its three suns.

*   *   *

Rebeeka was going through one of its periodic civil wars when Katie arrived, although there didn't seem to be anything terribly civilized about it from what she could see. Rebel strongholds in the snow-covered foothills near the spaceport fired several missiles at her while she was coming in to land. Fortunately, they were intercepted by Government anti-missile laser batteries before they could trigger any of the hidden modifications that she had bought on the black market to protect her ship in some of the more dangerous reaches of the cosmos. With the firepower she carried she could probably end the civil war right there and then, but they seemed to be having fun, and she didn't want to interfere.

The feathered Customs and Immigration officials at the spaceport tried to play down the attack, reassuring her that she was never in any danger. They obviously wanted to keep the tourists and the business-beings coming, but the bullet-holes in the walls and the boarded up windows weren't making their story easy to believe. The officials, eager to please, told her that the Rebeekan she was looking for — the latest and, she hoped, next-to-last possessor of the manuscript had

127

arrived on the planet a few weeks before. It had given its place of residence as a small hotel in the capital city, too far away to walk but not far enough to take a short trip in her ship.

Reluctant to take a cab, she returned to the ship and retrieved an antique Italian Lambretta moped from storage. Wrapping herself in several layers of clothing to keep out the bitter cold, she set off.

The journey to the capital city took forty minutes, and much of that was spent swerving round holes in the road left by mortar fire or car bombs. The hotel had been strafed by laser fire, some time in the recent past, but fortunately a bell-bird who still made a nest in the ruins told her that an elderly historian had been staying there until shortly before the strafing, but had managed to find an apartment a few streets away thanks to the accidental shooting of its previous occupants in a skirmish between Government forces and rebels.

She made her way cautiously to the address the bell-bird gave her, having to detour several times on the way to avoid barricades. The apartment block was still there when she arrived, which was an unexpected bonus as far as Katie was concerned. The place smelled of smoke and rotting vegetables. Most Rebeekans were staying off the streets, but behind shuttered windows she could see movement, and the sound of laughter and song drifted down to where she stood. Life went on, she supposed, even though war was all around. The sky was webbed with vapour trails, and there was a reddish glow on the horizon that either meant sunset was on the way or that part of the city was in flames. Unkindly, she hoped it was the latter.

The power seemed to be off, judging by the lack of any lights on the streets or behind the shutters, and she didn't fancy trying to find her way back to the spaceport in darkness. She shivered, despite the layers of clothing she wore. What the hell did she think she was doing? She found the apartment on the third floor of the block, having carried her Lambretta up the stairs in case some looter took a fancy to it out on the street.

She knocked on the door. Somewhere behind it, she heard a scuffling sound. She knocked again.

"My name is Katie Forrester," she called. "I'm a human, an archaeologist. I'm looking for a historian who was on a ship called the Arboline Queen until recently. I was given your name by a Karnite passenger."

After enough time had passed to convince her that she was going to have to adopt another strategy — one that might, on a less fraught world, be described as breaking and entering — the door suddenly opened. A small, ostrich-like figure wearing a threadbare suit and with a shock of white plumage on its head stood in the gap, silhouetted by a flickering glow in the room behind.

"My friend the Karnite," it said. "Yes, we had some good times together on that ship. I was so looking forward to seeing the planet poised between three suns, but then came news of the civil war, and I had to return.

My family..." It trailed off, shaking its head.

"My apologies," Katie said, "but I'm trying to track down a manuscript. It was written by a human who was either marooned or hiding - I'm still not sure - on a planet with no name. His ship travelled there through a wormhole, backwards in time. He lived for many years with a tribe who were descended from a human colony but who had forgotten their origins. The planet was used as a transit point by a multi-dimensional race called the Vethkin. I'm trying to find that manuscript. I traced it from Earth to Alpha Centauri, from Alpha Centauri to Ghazar, from Ghazar to Jullat, from Jullat to the Arboline Queen and then to here. Please, please tell me that you brought the manuscript here."

"l did," the Rebeekan confirmed. "You had better come in."

The room was bare, bereft of even the smallest scrap of furniture. A large drum stood in the centre. Flames licked over the top, and the metal sides radiated heat all around. "The power has been out ever since the rebels blew up the reactors," her host said, gesturing her to a space over in one corner where it had formed a sort of nest from blankets and sheets.

"I've burned everything I own to keep warm, and to cook my food. I only have one thing left to burn, and then I will either freeze or starve."

"The manuscript?" Katie said hopefully.

"My clothes," the Rebeekan answered. "l burned

the manuscript three days ago."

"Of course you did," Katie said automatically, although she felt despair and a huge weight of exhaustion pushing down on her.

"It was of little intrinsic value. What I had originally thought were fragments of some artistic effort were, in the end, merely doodles made by the writer. And I understand from my colleague the Karnite that there was no sociological or historical information in the manuscript that was not already known. It could provide nothing, apart from heat enough for me to live another night, and to cook a few scraps of meat with. Why are you so interested?"

"Because I think it was written by my father," Katie said quietly. "And because, if I am right, it would be the only thing I have left that he has ever touched with his own hands, and the only clue as to where he is now."

"Ah," said the Rebeekan. Together, they watched the sparks and smoke drift upwards from the fire, each trying not to think about the emptiness that, for different reasons, the future held for them.

ONLY CONNECT

James Willaker knew something was wrong when the taxi driver took him to a road that didn't exist.

It was his own fault. Later, in that brief period between his world being broken into pieces and then returning to normal again, he took some measure of comfort in that. The driver had made an honest mistake: Willaker had given him the wrong street name, the name of a street that hadn't been built yet, and the driver, assuming Willaker knew what he was talking about, took him there. It was that simple.

It was dark when he left the office: dark and raining. He'd been working overtime, poring over a high-definition computer screen, pulling up maps of the new Greenfen housing development and checking the cob-web-like overlays of sewage and water pipes, electrical conduits and fibre optic cables. Deconflicting the various elements of the development was a major headache, especially since the entire thing was going to be built on reclaimed marshland near the river and the surveyors couldn't guarantee the stability of the ground for anything more than five years. He'd spent most of the day rotating the three-dimensional view, peering at it from various angles and dragging the lines around, trying to ensure no element came within two metres of another. Not that it mattered: the builders would put things where they damn well wanted to regardless of whatever plans they were given. Sometimes Willaker wondered what his function actually was in the firm. Nothing ever got built according to the plans he drew up. Just like bus timetables gave bus companies a reason to be late, he suspected his plans were a blueprint for how a housing development *should* have been built.

He'd been vaguely aware of his colleagues turning their computers off, locking their in, out and pending trays away in their cupboards, putting their coats on and bidding each other goodnight, but it had been something in the background, like telephones ringing in real life filtering into the dreams of a sleeping mind. He was absorbed into a vision of multi-coloured lines weaving together to form the skeleton of a new town. By the time he woke up and looked around, the room was empty and his finger ached with the strain of holding the mouse buttons down. Time to go home.

He saved the files, turned the computer off, locked his desk drawers and slipped on his leather jacket. Rain splattered on the black mirror of the window as he avoided the gaze of his reflection. He was in his thirties, but his scalp showed through his hair if he stood with light in the wrong place and his skin had the dead whiteness of someone who hadn't seen daylight for a while. He tugged his collar up and adjusted the lapels. He wanted to look like Harrison Ford in *Blade Runner*, but he had a terrible feeling he looked more like Flash Harry the spiv in the *St. Trinian's* films.

As soon as the lift doors opened he sprinted across the lobby, rucksack hanging from one shoulder, hoping the security guard wouldn't see him before he got out of the building.

" 'Scuse me, sir!"

Damn. He turned, his fingers on the door handle.

The guard marched toward him, a smile on his face. His buttons were little brassy lights scattered across his uniform. "Big weekend coming up, sir. Three hundred of us in full armour doing the battle of Bosworth Field. You going to be there, sir?"

He shook his head, knowing how fake his smile must have looked. "No. No, I'm going out. Sorry." As the guard opened his mouth to start another conversation, Willaker quickly muttered, "Got to go – train to catch," and scooted out.

As the doors slid shut behind him and the rain pricked at his face, he glanced back. The guard's face had fallen into tragic lines, like a puppy who'd had his chewy bone snatched away. Willaker shrugged apologetically at him through the glass door. He felt guilty, but not guilty enough to go back in and talk. The man was an obsessive historical re-enactment buff who spent his every spare moment making armour and practising swordplay. Willaker had made the mistake of asking him one Monday morning what sort of weekend He'd had, and had spent the next half hour locked into a one-sided conversation about how the man had been taking part in a Viking assault on a castle in Kent and beat some poor Saxon black and blue with the flat of his axe blade. All Willaker had done was to make appreciative noises and run away the moment a dispatch rider provided a convenient distraction, but ever since then the guard had treated Willaker like a bosom buddy, assuming that he shared the same interests.

He shook his head and let his eyes wander away from the guard and across the facade of the building. It was a truncated pyramid built out of orange stone and tinted glass. Spotlights illuminated its Aztec facade. The Managing Director had designed it himself, and every time Willaker looked at it he wondered why anyone ever employed the firm

The walk home took half an hour on a good day, and there was precious little shelter from the rain, but he hated taking the bus. He had the kind of face that made people insist on telling him the story of their lives. Old women would detail the horrors of their recent varicose vein operations, while men in old, stained shirts would explain how they left plastic bottles full of water on top of their televisions so that, if the sets caught fire, the plastic would melt and put the fire out. And he would listen, nodding in the right places, counting the bus stops until he could get off.

He couldn't face it tonight, not after the security guard had already started things off. He'd get a taxi.

There was a café just opposite the building: a space between two buildings that had been roofed with sheets of corrugated iron and fronted with peeling wooden boards. The taxi drivers often stopped there for a cup of tea and a bite to eat. Willaker had never been inside – he usually made his sandwiches the night before and ate them at his desk – but he had often hailed a taxi outside as the driver was pulling away. Two cars were parked outside, their outsize aerials vibrating as the rain beat against them. Willaker checked the road for traffic then sprinted across to the other side, rucksack held up to ward off the rain.

The door banged open and two men emerged in a blare of light, smoke and noise. One of them turned and shouted something at the people still inside as his companion held the door open. Willaker's gaze flickered between them: which one to go for? Which one was less likely to make small talk?

The man holding the door was stuffing a bacon sandwich into his mouth with his other hand. His fingers gleamed with grease. He hadn't shaved for a few days. The other man, now turning away from the café and glancing over at Willaker, was tall, with short pepper-and-salt hair and a linen jacket that had seen better days worn over a loose shirt and chinos. He had a hipster beard. He looked more like a bohemian student than a taxi driver. He grinned at Willaker, and his entire face seemed to light up.

"Are you free?" Willaker asked him.

The man glanced over at his companion, who shrugged. Turning back to Willaker, he nodded. "Looks that way. Where would you like to go?

Geographically, I mean, not philosophically. I'm afraid I don't go south of Immanuel Kant on a Friday night."

It had been a long day. That was his only excuse. The phrase *Mallard Close* had been on the computer screen in front of him throughout his marathon subterranean mapping session. It didn't matter that he lived in a first floor flat in Curmore Road and that building wasn't scheduled to start on the Greenfen development for another six months: he was tired, and the first words to come out of his mouth were "Mallard Close, please."

The taxi driver grinned. "Mallard Close it is." He headed for the second car, a Peugeot that gleamed red under the neon streetlights.

Willaker waited until the driver unlocked the passenger door, and then climbed in. He glanced out of the window while the man started the car. The other man, the one with the bacon sandwich, was staring after them with a frown on his face. He took a step forward, as if to ask them something, and then thought better of it. Shaking his head, he walked toward his own car.

They pulled out and accelerated along the road. Street lights flickered past in an increasing rhythm, and Willaker suddenly felt the weight of the day descend on him. If he phoned out for a take-away and had a bath while he was waiting for it to arrive, then he could eat it in bed while watching *Newsnight*. A couple of bottles of beer to settle his stomach and he could be asleep by eleven.

"Can I take it that you've had a long day?" the taxi driver asked without turning his head away from the road.

"Yeah," Willaker muttered.

"Slaving over a hot computer screen?"

"Yeah," he replied. Conscious that he might have sounded rude, he added, "pretty late. Not as late as some nights."

The driver shook his head. Willaker noticed that he drove with one hand on the steering wheel and the other on the gear stick. His name and his photograph were stuck to the glove compartment cover in a laminated cover. John Smith. Driver number 2286. "So what is it that you do?" the man asked. "For a living?"

"I'm an architect."

John Smith nodded, smiling. "Ah, an architect. Humans will always need buildings, won't they? Civilizations and religions rise and fall, art forms come in and out of fashion, but people will always need somewhere to put their pot plants."

"That's right," Willaker muttered. "We're filling a basic human need for mezzanine floors and concealed lighting."

Driver number 2286. Willaker frowned. Surely the cab firm couldn't really employ over two thousand drivers. Maybe they had two offices, two sets of numbers, one set starting at one thousand and the other at two thousand. Or maybe they got through staff at an astounding rate and they didn't bother reassigning old numbers.

John Smith took a tight corner as neatly as if the car was on rails. "It must be very interesting, a job like that," he said over his shoulder. "You must have some stories – things that you wanted to build but couldn't, or things that looked great on the plans but went badly wrong when they were being constructed."

Willaker glanced out of the window, and a sudden spasm of panic gripped his heart as he failed to recognise the road they were driving down. It seemed to be on the outskirts of an industrial estate: the saw-tooth silhouette of a factory stood out against the rain clouds on one side while a chicken-wire fence protected a stretch of waste ground on the other. He'd never been there before, but somehow he recognised it. Strange, yet familiar.

It certainly wasn't on the way to Curmore Road.

"So what's the strangest thing that's ever happened to you?" the driver asked cheerfully.

Willaker disregarded the question, which sounded like it came from a textbook on *How to Entertain Your Passenger*. Concrete posts flickered in the corners of his eyes. "Are we going the right way?" he asked, an edge of panic in his voice.

Ahead, the road terminated in a circle of tarmac and a wire gate. A sign on stilts had been erected behind the gate, saying *Greenfen Housing Development*. The planned start date in smaller letters underneath was six months away. Willaker's firm got a credit as architects.

John Smith brought the car to a fast stop, took it out of gear and looked sideways at Willaker for the first time. "You wanted Mallard Close, didn't you?" He jerked a thumb at the fence. "Well, we're here."

"I wanted Curmore Road," Willaker said heavily.

John Smith shook his head. "You said Mallard Close. I'm sure of it."

Thinking back, Willaker knew he was right. He could hear himself saying the words. He was tired, He'd been thinking about Mallard Close all day, it was an easy mistake to make.

But that didn't explain...

"Maybe I did," he said, conceding the point with a slight nod of his head, "but Mallard Road doesn't exist."

The driver frowned. "What do you mean?"

"I mean, how did you know where Mallard Close is going to be? The names of the roads in this development were only suggested yesterday at an internal meeting of our company. The minutes haven't been written up yet, and it'll be weeks before the names are ratified. How do *you* know where Mallard Close is going to be built before we've even told the council?"

John Smith's face didn't react, but his gaze darted away from Willaker and toward the gate. "I... I believe I heard about it. Some of the other drivers were talking over a cup of tea and a bacon roll."

A fierce curiosity swept over Willaker. "Uh-uh.

Try again."

John Smith smiled and shrugged. "Perhaps I saw it on a map?"

"It's not on any maps," Willaker snapped. "At least, not on any printed ones."

"It is where I come from."

"And where's that, then?" He leaned forward aggressively.

"The future." There was still a smile on John Smith's face, but it was a different smile. A dangerous smile.

For a few moments Willaker couldn't understand what the man had said. He knew the meanings of the words, but he couldn't see how they applied to the conversation. John Smith might just as well have said "applecart furiously" or "goose wardrobe". Then the jigsaw piece slotted into place and he laughed. "The future? You mean you're a time traveller?"

John Smith nodded.

Glancing around the shabby interior of the car, Willaker said scathingly, "And I suppose this is your time machine, hmm?"

"Don't be foolish," John Smith replied, "this is a Peugeot."

Willaker blinked rapidly a couple of times. "Okay. Fine. What's the fare so far, then? I'll just get out and..."

"And what? You're right, my friend, Mallard Close hasn't been built yet. That was my mistake. With millennia to play around in, the odd decade here or there doesn't seem important. Of course, that's what a friend of mine said to Walter Raleigh on the day of his execution when he thought he was turning up for his wedding, but that's another story." He shook his head sadly. "It's always the little things that trip you up."

"My God, you're *serious*, aren't you?"

"I'd better drive you home. If I let you out here then you've got a long walk back, and this is an isolated spot. Nobody will be passing who could give you a lift."

"Except another time traveller," Willaker said. He meant it to be sarcastic, but the words came out sounding resigned.

John Smith shot him a wide-eyed look as he reached for the gear stick. "You're taking this very calmly. Aren't you going to tell me I'm insane?"

Willaker opened his mouth to say something, then closed it again and swallowed. Somewhere in the depths of his mind, he knew it was the only explanation that really fit the evidence. Oddly, of all the things that might have convinced him, it was the casual mention of Walter Raleigh. That could have been part of the man's madness, of course, but John Smith had just chucked it into the conversation without apology or ex-planation. He obviously believed it himself.

"A few years back," he said finally, "a French electronic rock musician named Jean-Michel Jarre played a concert in the London Docklands -"

"It's all right," John Smith interrupted. "You don't have to explain who Jean-Michel Jarre is. I'm reasonably *au fait* with classical music."

Willaker nodded. "Right. Okay." He gathered his thoughts together. They had a nasty tendency to keep falling apart and leaving him dazed. "It was an open-air concert with the most amazing light show you've ever seen - laser beams shining up onto the clouds, images projected onto buildings, all that and his music as well." He paused, remembering. "I was a student at the time, studying architecture and design, and I couldn't afford a ticket. Besides, I was more of a classical concert goer. Anyway, I was driving back from lectures to my digs in Catford when I suddenly crested a hill and saw this incredible multi-coloured glow from down by the river, this blaze of unearthly light that pulsed and danced in time with a deep rumbling." He laughed. "I thought a UFO had landed. For a second or two, I really thought a UFO had landed down by the river. "This is it!" I thought. "This is the year we make contact with aliens." Then I realised it was just a French rock musician and his light show, and I felt so... so disappointed. Stupid, huh?" He shook his head. "Look, can we talk? Can I... can I ask you some questions?"

"Would you like a cup of tea? I could drive us back to the café. There are no problems in life that can't be solved over a cup of tea."

"Yeah, that would be great, but look, I don't want to take you away from your job." He caught himself.

"Your driving job, I mean. I assume you've got another agenda as well."

"Don't worry. This sort of thing is what I'm here for."

"What sort of thing?"

"Talking. Listening."

"But –" Willaker's mind was racing ahead of his words, and he had to take a deep breath to calm himself down "—but aren't there any rules about, you know, giving things away?"

"What sort of things?" John Smith looked confused.

"The future."

He laughed as he reversed the car into a turn. "It doesn't work like that. I'll explain it all when we get back to the café."

The car raced off into the darkness. Willaker gazed out at the jagged shape of the factory roof, his mind flickering between belief and disbelief, awe and worry. Was he being suckered? Was John Smith just stringing him along, playing on his credulity?

He didn't think so. He really didn't think so.

The city built itself up around the moving car: hoardings replacing fencing, walls replacing hoarding, houses replacing factories. It was getting late. Public houses were beacons of light on street corners.

The car drew up in the same place it had left less than fifteen minutes before. The other car was gone, its bacon sandwich-eating driver with it.

"Come on," John Smith said, getting out. He was, Willaker realised, well over six feet tall. "This place serves the second-best tea I've ever tasted."

The café was long and thin. The floor was covered in stains and the tables were topped with chipped Formica. A dozen men were present, alone or sitting in pairs. A few of the pairs were playing cards. Half way along one wall, a counter had been built around a serving hatch. A gleaming metal tea urn and a plastic display case full of buns sat on the counter. The man behind the counter looked as if he had been a wrestler in a previous existence. Did places like this really exist any more? It was like going back –

– in time. Willaker smiled at the sudden thought, but underneath the smile he detected the sharp edge of hysteria. He took a deep breath.

"Annex a table," John Smith said, walking off toward the counter. "I'll get the tea."

Willaker sat down and tried not to display too much curiosity. He wondered how many of the men there were time travellers. If any. If the whole thing hadn't been run up out of whole cloth just for his benefit.

"Here you are," John Smith said, placing a mug of tea in front of Willaker. He put his own mug down, then turned his chair around and straddled it. Folding his arms across the back, he gazed at Willaker out of soulful brown eyes. "Let's cut to the chase – I'm a student of history and I've travelled back in time. I drive a taxi because it's one of the best ways to study history that I've found. Does that answer a lot of your initial questions?"

Willaker's mind freewheeled for a moment or two. "Historian?" he said stupidly. "Driving a taxi?"

John Smith smiled. "What is history?"

Surreal. This conversation was surreal. It occurred to Willaker that he might have gone mad, had a stroke, been hallucinating, anything.

Did it matter? Would it change the things he was doing if he suddenly realised he was barking mad?

"History," he said carefully, "is what happens. It's events. Wars. Treaties. Dates, times and places."

John Smith shook his head. "No. History is people. All the things you mentioned, they all boil down to what people do to other people. The trouble is that after a thousand years the people and what they did have boiled away, and what you're left with is the dry residue." The precision of the words clashed with his cheerful face and his casual clothes. He looked down at his tea. "If I leave this mug here and come back in a week or so, and if it's not been cleared away by Fred over there, then what's left in the bottom is what's left of history when you take the people out."

"And that's…?"

"That's what I'm doing here. That's what we're all doing here. Anecdotal history. Straight from the horse's mouth, as it were."

Willaker glanced round surreptitiously. "How

many people here are time travellers?"

John Smith calmly glanced from face to face. "Five. Six, perhaps."

"That many?"

"Have you never wondered why there are so many taxi drivers in London? Have you ever wondered why they're so talkative? Some are real, of course, but a lot of us are doing it for the stories."

"Is there really that much history to collect?"

"Absolutely, and it will all be lost if we don't collect it." He sipped his tea. "Who was the first American to engage the Japanese in combat at Pearl Harbour?"

Willaker shrugged. "I don't know. Some navy pilot, I assume. Does it matter?"

"It did to him. His name was Ray Buduick. He was a civilian, he lived in Honolulu and he owned a light aircraft. Nice man, by the way. Owned an Alsatian. On Sunday the seventh of December, he decided to take his plane up for a spin. Lovely day, he thought. Skies should be pretty clear. Of course, that morning they were full of Japanese Zeros who opened fire on him. They shot him up, but he managed to get away by banking steeply and they carried on to attack the naval base. He landed safely in the middle of the greatest airborne attack ever mounted."

"Is that true?" Willaker asked, amazed.

"As sure as I'm sitting here talking to you. I drove a cab in Maui for a while, and I heard the story from enough people, including Ray himself, that I'm positive it's true." He shrugged. "Everybody knows about Pearl Harbour, but who knows about Ray Buduick? As far as I'm concerned, he's as much an important historical character as President Eisenhower."

"But —" Willaker shook his head. "That sort of thing... it's *incidental*. I mean, it might be interesting, or funny, or sad, or whatever, but it's not *important*."

"You're missing the point. The fact that Hitler or President Reagan did something on a particular date isn't as important as the fact they both consulted an astrologer before they did it. History isn't a list of events, minute after minute, day after day, year after year - it's a web of people and the way they react to each other." He thought for a moment. "Look, a while ago I was in New York, driving a Yellow cab. I got chatting to a policeman one night. He was on his way home from the night shift. I asked him about his job - what it was like, what was the worst thing He'd ever seen, that sort of thing. Do you know what he told me? He said that there's an entire civilization of people living beneath the streets of New York, in the subway tunnels. He told me that they almost never come up to the surface, and that some of them are albino and blind, they've been down there for so long. He told me that they know the secret passages beneath New York — the abandoned subway lines, the tunnels built for gas and hydraulic lines that aren't used any more, the boarded-up basements and cellars that nobody knows exist, the sewers, and he told me how to find some of them. And that's what I do – I and the others here, the others like me. I collect these stories. I listen. I don't ask what *happened*: I ask what it was *like*."

There was silence after he finished talking. Willaker stared at him. For a moment he could see what John Smith was driving at: an organic view of time as an infinite series of connections between people. Something vibrant and alive, rather than the sterile series of dry facts He'd been taught at school.

"So where do I fit in?" he asked. "Why are you spending time talking to me? Am I part of history too? I've never done anything special. I probably never will."

"You're part of history," John Smith replied softly, "whether you like it or not. Whatever you do, whatever you say, you've made history. When the Greenfen Housing Development is built, you'll be one of the few people who know its secrets."

"But it hasn't got any secrets," Willaker said. "It's one of the most boring projects I've ever worked on."

"There must be something unusual about it."

"Well some crazy old woman came into our office last month telling us to stop the project."

"Go on."

"Said that her family had been living here for generations, and there was a story that her grandmother told her, something about the bodies of plague victims having been dumped into the marsh in the seventeenth century. We checked. All records had been lost, but - " he glanced around warily, " – when we did some exploratory digging we came up with some really old bones."

"So what did you do?"

"We assumed we'd found some dog bones, we filled in the holes we'd dug and we carried on as if nothing had happened. We'd invested too much time and money into the project to have a full-scale archaeological dig shut it down for five years." He looked into his tea. "But they didn't look like any dog bones *I'd* ever seen."

The driver nodded. "You see – if I hadn't been here, talking to you, that information would have been lost. Nobody would ever have known about that plague pit."

"For God's sake," Willaker said, "don't tell anyone I told you. I'll be fired!"

"Don't worry, my friend. By the time I record this information, the Greenfen development will be long gone."

Willaker felt a sudden tight sensation in his throat, and he had to look away before John Smith saw the way his eyes had filled with tears. For a long while his life had been empty and meaningless, like a road going nowhere under an overcast sky. John Smith's words had opened up a rift in the clouds through which the sun was shining. He'd never thought of it that way before, but Smith was right. He *was* a part of history. He *was* a part of that web, connected to everyone and everything, from kings to beggars, from birth to death.

He had to change the subject before he started crying. "Do you tell everyone you talk to you're a time traveller?" he asked. "Or am I just lucky?"

"Not usually," John Smith replied. "I made a foolish mistake with you, and I felt I owed you an explanation."

"I asked earlier whether you were worried about giving things away about the future and changing time, and you said you'd explain it later. Won't it affect things, me knowing that time travel is possible? Isn't there a chance I might do something different now, something I wouldn't have done before? What if my house would have caught fire if I went home, but because you told me you're a time traveller and because I came here with you, I'm still alive? Won't that sort of thing change the future?"

John Smith half smiled, and shook his head sadly. "Time doesn't work like that. You're confusing time and history. History's the one like a web of connections. Time's not like that at all. You know that there are elemental particles that matter is built up of? Well, time's the same. There's a smallest possible unit of time, indivisible and complete. We call them 'moments'. You can change time, moment by moment, but as soon as you stop changing it, the next moment that comes along will be the same as it was before. Unless you make a really big change, and then you drag time off course, but that's a thing we try not to do if we can help it. It's like – " he thought for a moment, " – it's like a computer hard drive. Let's say you're writing a novel – the longest novel ever written. Far bigger than all of *Harry Potter* put together. It's all there, saved on your hard drive as a massive string of binary digits. Then, while you're asleep, someone sneaks into your flat and rewrites chapter five so the main character dies. That doesn't affect the rest of the book. That character is still alive in chapter six, and all the subsequent chapters. Only chapter five has changed." He shrugged. "Time is the same. Just because a few moments have been rewritten, it doesn't mean that everything after those moments gets rewritten as well. Time resets itself as if nothing had happened. You will forget me, and what we talked about, as if it never happened." He glanced at the clock behind the counter. "But I digress. It's time I was getting back on the road."

"But – can't we keep talking?" Willaker asked desperately. "There must be a lot of things I can tell you."

The driver shook his head, smiling sadly. "Alas, no. Now that you know who I am, anything you might tell me is contaminated. You'll naturally self-edit and adjust what you say, emphasising some things and playing down others. That's one of the rules we play to – stories have to come naturally, told to us as if we're just another person you've bumped into." He stood. "It's been nice chatting to you. Good luck. One of the chaps here will take you home. Don't ask him if *he's* a time traveller – he might not be. And if he is, he won't admit it."

As John Smith walked off toward the café door, Willaker was frozen for a moment. The hairs on the back of his neck began to bristle. "Wait!" he called after him, "what about me? What happens now?"

But John Smith was gone.

By the time Willaker finished his tea the rain had stopped. He looked around, still holding the cup. He had a feeling He'd been talking about something, but he couldn't remember what. And who could he have been talking to? One of the drivers? The man at the counter? That didn't seem like him at all.

Back in his flat, with a takeaway dished out on a large plate, he picked up the remote from the side of the bed and turned the television on. Colours swam up from the darkness of the screen: tiny figures kicking a ball across an unnaturally green background. The changing light levels cast flickering shadows across his bedroom. He changed channels just in time to catch the opening credits of *Newsnight*. Depending on how interesting the headlines were, He'd watch it while he was finishing his takeaway then settle down to sleep.

And then the office tomorrow, and more long hours moving lines around a screen, followed by a takeaway maybe a DVD. Next day: the same. It didn't matter what John Smith had said. Once upon a time, when Willaker was a student, he'd dreamed of making a difference, making his mark on history. He'd dreamed that he would design buildings that would live on as a monument to his name, but he knew now that history was passing him by and he would be forgotten, even before he died.

He leaned over and reached for bedside cabinet. The light from the television reflected back as an amber glow from the bottle of whisky inside. His fingers closed around the comforting weight of the bottle.

History had forgotten about him. With enough whisky inside him, he could forget about history.

THE OLD, OLD STORY

Winter had stayed like an unwelcome guest long into spring that year. Snow still carpeted the mountain slopes and the steep roofs of the houses, and the cold winds blowing across from the steppes carried nothing before them but the promise of more. Each day the icy surface of the well had to be broken anew. Murzasichle, high in Poland's gaunt Carpathian Mountains, survived on cooperation and friendship, and the memories of other times like these.

Father Pradziad struggled upwards through the crisp white shroud which covered the hillside. Far beneath him the cabins of the village were sliced into a brightly painted mosaic by the forest. Ahead the spruce trees stood like charcoal marks on paper, their lines abbreviated by the harsh wind and the cold. The constant, dazzling whiteness made distances hard to judge and, with the black slashes of the trees seeming to dance against the bright backdrop of snow, Father Pradziad was hard-pressed even to tell which direction was uphill.

The only sounds were the muffled crunch of snow beneath his boots and the distant chugging of the snowplough as it tried to keep the main road to Zakopane open. The bitter smell of pinecones filled the cold air. The heavy hem of his cloak dragged behind him, erasing his trail as he went. He checked his wristwatch and struggled faster through the drifts, knowing that if he failed to return to the village before night fell he risked losing his way in the forest. It was possible to find his way back by other means, but he did not want to be forced to use them.

Ahead, through the trees, Pradziad recognized the house of Franek Szulc. Gratefully the priest moved faster, desperate to rid himself of the ice-goblins which nibbled hungrily at his fingers.

Before his outstretched hand could even touch the door it was pulled open, and the bearlike figure of his friend was welcoming him into the blessed warmth of the chalupa' s black room. He barely noticed his cloak being removed and hung by the door. The sight of the glowing logs in the fireplace filled his eyes, and the crackling as they split and burned almost drowned out Szulc's voice. The smoke stung his nostrils, and the flames reminded him, as they always did, of other times, long ago.

"Andrzej, at last!" boomed Szulc as he manoeuvred the priest into the large central room of the house. His wife Ewelina squeezed past her husband as Father Pradziad lowered himself thankfully into an armchair by the fire. She was small and fragile beside Szulc, like a porcelain figure glazed with the hairline cracks of middle age. Her blouse was as white as the snow outside. Her dress was black, embroidered with tiny flowers in scarlet and gold. Szulc flung an affectionate arm around her shoulder. She shrugged him off, but smiled as she did it.

"You'll take food with us, of course," she said, gazing fixedly like a sparrow up into the priest's face.

"I really shouldn't..." Father Pradziad began to say, but she was already heading towards the kitchen.

Szulc's hand closed over his shoulder. "None of this nonsense," he said, "Andrzej will eat with us – won't you Andrzej?"

"Franek, I couldn't possibly – "

" – Offend my hospitality by refusing my food," finished Szulc, smiling as he played the role of *nukak*, the one who urges.

Father Pradziad smiled back. Honour had been satisfied on both sides.

"I found your note when I returned from Zakopane," he said. "I came as soon as I could. What troubles you, my friend?"

Szulc slumped heavily into a chair. "What took you to Zakopane?" he asked, avoiding the priest's gaze.

Pradziad hesitated before he answered, feeling his way through the conversation. Whilst he tried to identify the source of the Szulcs' worries, Ewelina emerged from the kitchen, her tray piled high with meats, smoked cheeses, and pickled mushrooms. The aromas mingled with the smell of wood smoke, and Pradziad began to realize how hungry he was. Ewelina placed the tray on a small table to one side and retreated back to the kitchen.

"A child whose parents claimed she was

possessed," he replied eventually. "Nothing more than epilepsy. I recommended the hospital in Warsaw."

"You seem to spend a great deal of time traveling. We see so little of you here in Murzasichle."

"There are so few in the Church these days who believe in the power of evil. I seem to have become something of a specialist in possession. He smiled benignly. "What ails you, Franek?" he said again.

"It's little Anatoly," said Szulc, shifting in his chair. "When he's around... things happen." He buried his head in his hands. His wife, entered with a pot of sweet tea which, by the smell, was laced with vodka, placed it beside the food and stroked her husband's neck.

"Things?" the priest asked quietly. Ewelina Szulc looked at him, then looked away.

"It started a few weeks ago," she said. "Just after his twelfth birthday. He's been growing up so quickly these past few months. It's hard to believe..." She stopped abruptly. Her husband reached up and took her hand from his neck, cradling it gently in his. He looked up at Pradziad.

"We thought nothing of it at first," he said, quiet and level. "A few smashed cups, an overturned chair or two. We thought it was the dogs, or Anatoly and some of his friends in one of their boys' games. You know how it is when you're young?" Pradziad smiled in reassurance. Szulc squeezed ·his wife's hand briefly and paused, looking for the right words. "Then it got worse.

Plates were broken. One afternoon I came back from the village to find a window smashed and the glass outside in the snow."

Father Pradziad leaned forward and picked up his cup of tea. Reminded by the priest's action, Szulc did the same.

"Go on," said Pradziad.

"And then, one night, after Anatoly had gone to bed..."

"Yes?"

Szulc looked up at his wife. She smiled tightly and ·nodded. "I swear to God, Andrzej, we saw a teapot fly across the room and smash against the wall. And there wasn't a soul near it. Not a living soul!"

Father Pradziad looked down into his cup. The surface of the tea vibrated gently, forming small rings that fitted one inside another and vanished into the centre of the liquid.

"I don't disbelieve you, Franek," he began.

"It happened, Andrzej! I tell you, it happened!"

"And where is the lad now?"

Szulc looked to his wife, who touched his shoulder reassuringly.

"I sent him upstairs for a nap," she said. "He's been getting easily tired since..." She stopped, suddenly overcome by the sense of what she was saying.

"Since this all began," Szulc continued. He shook his head sorrowfully, and Pradziad noticed that his hand had begun to shake, clattering the teacup against the saucer. "The boy is possessed, Andrzej! You are our friend as well as our priest. Tell us what to do."

The priest leaned forward reassuringly and lay his hand upon his friend's wrist, hoping to calm him down, but to his surprise here was no tremor in Szulc's arm at all. Not a quiver. Szulc and his wife were both staring into the teacup with sick apprehension upon their faces. The cup clattered violently, moving up the curved side of the saucer and threatening to spill the hot liquid into Szulc's lap. The priest watched, amazed. Suddenly he noticed a slight vibration in his own hand. He glanced down, knowing what he would see. The surface of his tea was jittering in the cup like a rough ocean as the cup wandered aimlessly about in the saucer.

"Always when he's asleep," said Szulc. "After an hour or so."

Pradziad looked up into Szulc's eyes.

Thud!

Pradziad almost dropped his cup as the sound echoed around the small house. Ewelina burst into tears.

Thud! Thudthud! Thud!

Franek's hands clenched and unclenched. The strongest man in the village, he looked frail and tired, but not surprised.

Thudthudthud! Thud!

The sound was coming from upstairs. Pradziad could have sworn that he could see the carved spruce beam which supported the ceiling shake in its sockets.

"His bed," whispered Ewelina Szulc. Her eyes were dark and shadowed. "It's his bed."

"And he's still asleep?" asked the priest, aghast. Szulc merely nodded.

Father Pradziad reached out and took the hands of Franek md Ewelina Szulc. "Oh God, most merciful," he began, "hear us in our hour of need."

With an incoherent cry Ewelina Szulc, unable to take the strain any more, sprang to her feet and ran towards the stairway. Her husband tried to stop her, but she was too quick. With Franek and Father Pradziad close behind she stumbled up the stairs, but by the time she got to her son's bed room the noises had ceased.

Unable to see over Franek Szulc's shoulder, Father Pradziad peered under his arm. Young Anatoly slept peacefully in a tangle of linen, framed by his father's body. His face was puffy and flushed and his hair was slicked with sweat, yet he looked somehow still angelic and innocent in the light that spilled through the drawn curtains.

Could they be wrong? Pradziad wondered to himself. *Could he be just an ordinary boy?* Then he saw the circular dents that pockmarked the carpet around the legs of the boy's bed.

"Wake him," he said, harsher than he had intended. "I'll be waiting downstairs."

Concerned voices murmured behind him as he descended the stairs, and as he entered the main room he heard Anatoly's sleepy reply. He felt tired. Old and tired. This was the part he hated most about his chosen vocation; the rooting out of the unnatural, the inquisition, the penance. He had hoped that his time in Murzasichle would be free of such problems. He'd had enough. He wanted a rest.

"Father?"

He turned. Ewelina stood in the doorway, her face haggard, her hand on young Anatoly's shoulder. Franek stood behind him, filling the space.

Pradziad smiled warmly at Anatoly, but inside he was cold at the thought of what was to come.

"Anatoly," he said, "how large you've grown. I remember when I arrived in Murzasichle you were only," and he gestured vaguely with his hands, "this high. Look at you! You're almost a man now!"

Anatoly just stared back at the priest. His eyes had a bruised look to them, and his shirt was buttoned up awry.

Pradziad tried again. "I want you to take a walk with me into the woods," he said. "There are things we must talk about. Things," he added meaningfully, "I think you might *want* to talk about."

Anatoly frowned warily. "My father told me to keep out of the forest," he said. "He said there are wolves there."

Pradziad smiled benignly. "Trust me," he said. "We'll be safe."

"What about the *planetnicy*?" the boy replied

stubbornly.

"Stories, Anatoly, just stories. There are no demons, especially ones who move storm clouds around for fun. Not any more."

Anatoly looked up at his father for reassurance, but Franek Szulc merely patted his shoulder and said in a voice that was too hearty to be convincing, "You just go along with Father Pradziad, and don't worry about the wolves. Or the *planetnicy*. Father Pradziad is a man of God, and God will protect the both of you."

Anatoly didn't look convinced but, deprived of excuses, he held his arms away from his sides as his mother helped him into his coat.

"Take good care of him, Andrzej," Szulc murmured, and then added in a louder voice, "And you obey the Father, Anatoly, do you hear me?"

Anatoly Szulc nodded his head, then pulled on a pair of mittens and followed the priest toward the door.

Within a few minutes they had climbed far enough up the hill for the trees to hide the house and the village below. They could have been a hundred miles from Murzasichle. Snow covered everything around them like a fungal growth. It seemed to glow of its own accord, and both Pradziad and Anatoly had to screw their eyes into slits to avoid walking into bushes, trees or each other. The branches of the trees were burdened with snow, and for a moment it appeared to Pradziad that the white snow was actually the trees and the darker branches beneath merely shadows cast by the sun. But only for a moment.

Eventually Father Pradziad found a spot which, for reasons which he couldn't explain appealed to him as fitting. He brushed the snow from a fallen tree trunk and gestured to Anatoly to sit beside him.

"Can you guess why I wanted to talk to you?" he asked kindly.

The boy's face was as frozen as the land. Eventually he managed a tight little nod.

"Your mother and father are worried," Father Pradziad continued. "They fear for you."

"I haven't done anything wrong," the boy said.

"I know," said Pradziad, "I know. But nonetheless, they worry. They hear strange noises, and they see strange sights, and they think perhaps that their son has been possessed by demons." He smiled. "By *planetnicy* perhaps."

Anatoly's eyes filled with a sudden rush of tears. "Will you have to drive the demons out of me?" he asked breathlessly. "Will God hate me for ever and ever?"

"Can you say the Lord's Prayer?"

Anatoly frowned, remembering, then said in a rush; "*Pater noster, qui es in Caelis; sanctifictur nomen tuum –* "

Father Pradziad stopped him with a raised hand.

"You see?" he said, smiling. "If you'd been possessed by demons, you'd be nothing but a puff of black smoke by now."

The boy couldn't help smiling back. "So if I'm not possessed," he said, "then what am I?"

Pradziad stretched his arms out in front of him and then raised them above his head, easing the kinks in his back. The vertebrae in his neck and spine creaked arthritically.

"You feel out of place here, don't you?" he murmured sympathetically. "Like a stranger to your friends and your family."

The boy nodded, desperately eager to be understood and accepted, if only by his priest.

"Do you ever feel superior to them?" Father Pradziad asked, just as warmly. "Do you ever pity them, because they can't do the things that you can?"

Anatoly looked away, flushing suddenly despite the cold.

"I'll let you into a secret," Pradziad continued. "So do I. I'm not a mountain-liver, a *gorale*. I've lived here for ten years now, but I'll always be the new priest." He was looking beyond Anatoly flow, across the years and the miles of his life, and he wondered if Anatoly could detect an undertow of bitterness there. "We're outsiders, you and I. We have that in common.

The boy nodded, clearly unsure of the priest's meaning.

Pradziad trembled slightly as he pulled himself back from whatever thoughts had entangled him. He smiled warmly at Anatoly.

"You're not alone, young man," he said reassuringly. "There have been other people who can do the things that you can do. I've heard about them. I've made a point of seeking them out. You're only the third one I've ever found. It's a rare gift, you know? It's a capability that's been lost to humanity for thousands of years, apart from the occasional throwback like you. And like me."

Anatoly's face had broken into a hesitant smile, but his eyes were still shadowed. "I have dreams," he blurted, and looked up beseechingly into the priest's face. Pradziad nodded knowingly, and Anatoly continued with more confidence. "I dream that it's night and I'm flying through the sky, looking down on all of the houses and seeing all the little people inside. I dream that I've got wings!"

A shadow passed across his face.

"But when I try to see the wings they fold up beneath me and I can't fly any more, and_ I fall all the way to the ground. And then I wake up crying, and things are always smashed downstairs."

Pradziad patted the boy's shoulder.

"That's the first lesson I would have taught you," he said. "The wings are just for decoration. It's your mind that holds you up."

Anatoly frowned, confused by the priest's words.

"I've been so frightened," he whispered. "So scared."

Father Pradziad sighed, and looked beyond the boy. "Do you remember my sermon last week?" he asked.

The boy shook his head.

"No," the priest continued, "it was hardly the stuff of memories, was it? 'Now the serpent was more subtle than any beast of the field.' Hardly inspiring. And yet there's a lot of truth in the Bible, if you know where to look. In the old days, the peasants of China worshipped us and feared us. They thought that were gods who could take on human form. They didn't realize that we were humans with another form in our mind's eye, and the power to make that form real. Once in a generation, a child is born with the power. We used to teach them to use it. Now we kill them to stop them. It's just another chapter in an old , old story, my son," he said sadly, as a blush the colour of burnished gold spread across his skin, and his wings spread wide to eclipse the sun . "There isn't enough room in the world for all of us. A few can survive, h1idden in human bodies, but any new-born like you might draw attention to us."

His eyes were slits, and a long-banked fire was flaring behind him.

"In the old days we could have fought from sunrise to sunset and gloried in the battle, but times have changed. We have to catch you young now."

Anatoly screamed as a jewelled claw the size of his father's body reached out toward him.

*   *   *

Winter had stayed like an unwelcome guest long into spring that year. Snow carpeted the mountain slopes and the steep roofs of the houses, and it was a long time before the hot breath of the *halny* winds blew once again from the far Mediterranean. For weeks the valley had been filled with the tinkling of falling icicles d the slushy wet rush of snow sliding from the roofs and into the streets.

The remains of Father Pradziad were never discovered. Nobody in Murzasichle was surprised. By then everybody in the tillage had heard the story of how their priest and young Anatoly Szulc had been set upon as they were walking in the forest by wolves made ravenous by the cold, and how Father Pradziad had distracted the wolves away, giving Anatoly time to escape. Young Anatoly had become something of a celebrity, with people coming from as far afield as Nowy Targ and Zakopane to marvel at his story and at the calmness with which he recounted it.

Searches had been organized as soon as Anatoly ran into the village, of course but Anatoly could not remember where they had walked and who could blame him? Besides, winter had made its passing felt with unexpected flurries of snow, and any tracks would have been covered over within minutes of being made. Reluctantly, the search was abandoned. Despite the absence of a body, Father Pradziad's funeral took place after three days of weeping, feasting, praying and dancing. In death he had become what he always wanted to be – *gorale*.

Much to the surprise of Franek and Ewelina Szulc, the gift that had set young Anatoly apart from his friends seemed to vanish with the snows. They gave thanks to God and, when they visited the graveyard to pay-their respects to Father Pradziad's empty grave, they gave thanks to him as well.

Anatoly himself kept very quiet about that day on the mountain, priests who turned into *planetnicy*, and trees which mysteriously uprooted themselves and flew through the air to impale demons and save a young boy from death. On those increasingly frequent occasions when he awoke to find himself coasting silently through the starry sky, held aloft by the power of his mind and guiding his flight with vast, sail-like wings, he closed his eyes and wished himself back in bed.

He didn't want to call attention to himself.

From anything.

CRAWLING FROM THE WRECKAGE

There are cormorants nesting in the wreckage now. Even after all this time the islanders will still not come near it, and yet the cormorants quite happily hop in and out of the rents in its skin, mate there, lay their egg and raise their young.

It was less than a year ago that it carried me from the skies, burning and breaking apart around me, crashing onto the shore and letting the waves and the rain put out its fire. The storm was bad that night. The waves carved the shoreline and the dunes into new shape and threw me far up the beach toward the cliffs, to the point where the sea grasses thin out and the dunes begin.

r can remember only isolated fragments of that night now - the sea rushing lip to hit me, and flowing around my half-buried body; the waves retreating, gathering their strength for another assault on the beach; the crumpled struts of the wreckage emerging like the legs of an upturned crab beside me; the still form of an old woman staring down at me in the sanctuary of a cave. The last thing I saw was her weathered and immobile face; the last thing I heard was the pounding of the waves on the beach.

The sea can never reach the wreckage now: it lies rusted and inviolate above the line of seaweed that marks the tide. Sometimes it seems to me that the seaweed is a fence between the sea and the wreck, but whether it prevents the waves getting to the wreck or the wreck getting to the waves I do not know. But then, sometimes it seems that I can hear the cormorants calling to me with the voices of long ago friends, and then J know that I have been sitting for too long staring at the sea, and the wreck, and the sun.

I think the cormorants know me. I know that their voices are my creation rather than theirs, but I still believe that they have come to recognize me, accept me, and know that r am no threat. They certainly sec enough of me. I have my favourite spot, nestled between two steep-banked sand dunes close to the cliffs and protected from the wind and the wind-borne sea spray. From it I can see the wide sweep of the bay and the white caps to the waves that might be the foam as they curl and break, or the cormorants riding them and diving for food. The cormorants are mv friends: large birds with grey-brown feathers tipped in black, their beaks curved and cruel. They watch me as they sit on the remains of my craft and survey their isolated kingdom. They glance over, glitter-eyed and suspicious if I shift my position to ease the cramp in my joints. my leg still aches badly at high tide and during storms. The scars on my body have healed, but some injuries take longer. Once in a while I wake sweating, thinking I can hear tortured metal screaming. It is only the cormorants. Only ever the cormorants.

At least the islanders tolerate me now, although

the wreckage is outside their experience. They are unfamiliar with the principles of metalworking, although I have seen metal implements on the island, and the burnt, angular struts and crisped skin of the wreck must look to them like the bones of some huge dragon. Or perhaps I overestimate them. The islanders share many characteristics but imagination is not one of them. In a way they are as much outside my experience as the wreck is outside their. I am forced to accept what they do, how they think, without knowing why. They shun the wreck, but they do not avoid me. Not anymore.

It was in this spot where I now sit, in the notch between two dunes on the southern beach of the island, that Jethro claims he found me. Perhaps the old woman had dragged me back down the beach toward the wreck. Perhaps I imagined both her and the cave. Jethro later told me I had been unconscious and raving for a week while he bathed the wounds, so any memories I have before I woke up are suspect. My life, my new life, started at that moment.

Glancing up, I saw looming cliffs and heard the sound of waves, but the cliffs were Jethro's weatherworn feature and the waves were far away.

"You're safe," he said curtly. Faded blue eyes watched me for some sign of understanding. Behind him there was worn wood, and to my right a window. I could smell the sea. Cormorants were crying somewhere outside.

"How long... " I started to say, but my voice was dry and tasted of bile. Jethro eased me up from the mattress I was lying on and handed me an earthenware mug. I sipped the water gratefully.

"Six days," he muttered. "We found you on the beach up near the naming cave. You were injured, so Ruth and I brought you here. I'm Jethro."

"My name is Thomas," I whispered, raising my head weakly. "Thomas Jerome."

Jethro slid his hand beneath my neck to support me as I looked around. The furniture in the hut was handmade from driftwood and branches. There was no evidence of nails, only crude mortise and tenon joints holding it all together. The material from which the curtains and sheets had been made was a rough, homespun wool, patchily hand-dyed.

"Strange sort of wreckage," he said. "Never seen a boat like it. "

"It wasn't a boat," I whispered, "it was an aeroplane." His face creased along existing lines.

"A what?"

"An aeroplane." He still looked blank, and I started to wonder exactly how far I had flown. The storm had been brewing as I took off from my first refuelling stop at Dover, so this still had to be England, or, at the very least, an island off the coast. Aeroplanes had been around for enough years for them not to be a novelty, and since the Great War everybody who read a newspaper knew what one looked like.

"An aero... plane?" He tried the word hesitantly.

"A machine for flying in," I explained. My voice was firming up with use, but my throat still felt as if I had been gargling sand.

"Witchcraft," he muttered with a strange sort of wariness in his voice. "They talk about flying machines on the mainland. Never put much truck in mainland tales myself, considering what they say about us."

I suddenly realized how bad the throbbing in my head was, and with that realization the rest of my body clamoured for attention. My right leg ached and, looking down, I saw dried blood on my thigh. My chest and legs were covered in cuts and scratches, some rough and deep, some like doodled pencil lines, all of them clean and healing. I could understand the rough-edged scrapes – the spars and supporting members broken in the crash would have clawed at my body as I thrashed my way from the wreck – but the thin scrolling cuts confused me for a moment. I thought back to the last few moments of my old life, and remembered wires under tension suddenly snapping and lashing back into the cockpit, slicing through clothes and flesh alike, as the aircraft crumpled in the fist of the wind. It was not the end. There were bound to be boats, and from what Jethro had said the English coast was not that far away.

Jethro offered me the water again. I sipped in silence, watching the motes of dust that floated calmly on the surface. A shadow moved past the window, then the door opened and then Ruth walked in.

"How do you feel?" she asked, putting down the bundle of rags she carried and coming across to me. I pulled the sheet lip to cover my chest, acutely conscious of my nakedness. I tried to tell her how grateful I was for their care, but the words caught in my throat and I ended up gagging violently with both of them holding onto me. As the heaving subsided and they laid me gently back onto the bed, I found myself staring at Ruth. She was not beautiful – her face was too rounded, her eyes too foreign for that – but there was something natural and joyful about the way she moved that absorbed my attention. She was like no woman I had seen before.

"Do you feel strong enough to eat?" she asked. I nodded, suddenly aware that I was ravenous. "Fine. There's stew if you can manage it and bread as well."

The stew was thick and hot, made from vegetable and occasional chunks of fish, and we washed it down with sweet. dark beer that had been brewed in the village. There was a reserve in their manner at first. Jethro, in his rough island way, questioned me about where I had come from but relaxed when he realized that I was from further away than the immediate mainland. Somehow I gained the impression that there was bad blood there. a feud of some sort. Ruth sat on the end of my bed, holding Jethro's hand. He had pulled up a rough-hewn wooden chair in order to sit beside me.

They were both interested in my aeroplane. Ruth was inclined to dismiss it, first as a fanciful tale and then, when she realized that I was serious, as a trivial boy's toy of no practical value. Jethro asked me technical questions without knowing what words to use, and I found to my shame that my dependence on my mechanics had been more profound than I had realized. When he asked me what kept it up in the air, I found myself waffling about the cormorants and the curve of their wings. Jethro thought I was trying to make a fool out of him, and left in a temper. I was too bus. to care, wondering what I had been thinking of, setting off with a decrepit De Havilland DH16 on the long Right to Barcelona and the Spanish Civil War with a storm brewing and without the faintest idea of what to do if something went wrong. As, of course, it had.

Idealism can make fools of us all.

I slept for most of the next few days. When I woke either Jethro or Ruth was there with me, offering me food, or water, or a hand to hold. If it was night then it was Jethro. If the sun slanted in through the broken glass and the cormorants cried outside then it was Ruth. She was still living with her family at the time, but she and Jethro were betrothed, and she seemed to spend most of her time unchaperoned at his hut. I developed a slight fever again, not as bad as before but enough to blur another few days together in my mind. I can remember waking sometimes to find myself screaming in the middle of a nightmare as I relived the crash and the struggle to shore. Occasionally in my thrashing I reopened old wounds, and awoke to find the sheets smeared with blood.

Eventually I woke one morning soaked in sweat, but my mind was whole and mine once more and my body was weak but responsive. Jethro was there with me. I wolfed down breakfast - crusty black bread and water – and I could have eaten lunch right after. I felt complete, in control again. I felt like the man I had been before I crashed, and my thoughts turned to how I could leave. Jethro and I talked of generalities again: how I felt, what the weather was like, the prospects for a good harvest that year. Jethro always avoided asking me anything personal. He always left it up to me to talk, and I never did.

Instead I asked Jethro what he did, how he survived and earned the money to buy food and clothes for himself and Ruth. He went and stood by the window. I thought for a moment that he would not answer. His manner toward me was usually little better than wary, and sometimes downright suspicious.

"I weave nets for the fishermen," he said finally. "The storms are always pulling them onto the rocks and ripping them, so they come to me for repairs. Patched nets are never as good the second time around, so I usually end up making new one." He looked out at the cormorants. "My father taught me how to make them, and his father taught him. Trouble is, I don't know everything he knew, and he didn't know everything his father knew. Things change and never for the better."

I could see cormorants wheeling aimlessly in the sky past his head.

"And what about Ruth?" I asked.

"She looks after the old 'un," he said, then stopped, as if he had said too much,

"The old 'un?"

"The old 'un used to live in the village, long time ago now," he muttered eventually, "Decided she preferred it down on the beach, near where we found you, Only likes to be bothered for namings and…" he looked at me strangely, "marriages, Ruth looks after her needs,"

"I think I remember her, She pulled me to safety, I think, There was a cave…"

"Yes," Jethro said, "a cave."

The sun made a buttress against the shadows, bracing the windowed wall against the floor. Dust motes sparkled briefly a they danced lazily through the beam, Outside, the cormorants called to each other in a private tongue.

"I would like to express my gratitude," I said. 'Could we…"

"She won't see you."

"Even so…"

He sighed, and looked out of the window.

"Ruth's been on at me to get you up and about She reckons the exercise will do you good,"

He dug out some old, faded clothes to replace my ripped flying kit, and supported me as I stumbled down the rocky path to the beach to look over the wreckage, It was difficult to associate the broken struts and burnt, salt-caked skin with the graceful creature that had carried me through the sky, I felt nothing for her. Both of us had changed too much.

I looked around for the cave I remembered seeking sanctuary in, but the cliff face behind us was riddled with holes and fissures, none of which looked familiar, I made to move toward them but Jethro took my arm, His face was crinkled with concern and… could it be?.. fear.

"Best not," he said, "She doesn't take kindly to newcomers."

"But she saved my life!"

He frowned, and looked out at the calm grey sea. "I'm sure she had her reasons," he said quietly.

I wanted to ask more but Jethro turned and started back toward the path up to the hut. It was clear that he was going back, with me or without me, I looked back toward the cliff face. I thought I could see Ruth leaving one of the caves, but then Jethro called me, and I had to hurry to catch up with him.

We walked back in silence. My joints ached, but the sea air filled my lungs and invigorated me. My thoughts turned again to leaving, I would ask Ruth about the fishing fleet, and the mainland.

Back at the hut Jethro and I sat in uncomfortable silence for a while. After a time I could only measure by the movement of the sun across the floor, Ruth arrived with food. The atmosphere in the hut shifted in some subtle way as we ate lunch, and twice my eyes caught Ruth's across the space between us. Or perhaps my mind was still clouded with sleep and I misinterpreted the expression in her eyes. I still felt light-headed, and my joints ached, so when Ruth suggested we take a slow walk into the village and back I took little persuading. Jethro looked regretful, but said that he had some mending to do. The storm that interrupted my Right had also ripped many of the nets against the stone reefs that surrounded the fishing grounds. We walked out into the afternoon sunshine and took a path that wound through the grassy dunes and up the face of the small cliff. Jethro sat cross-legged in front of the hut, a diminishing Figure as we climbed together. Within five minutes he had faded into the heat haze.

The path to the village led up along the cliff top above the beach, and I could feel my muscles gratefully stretching, easing and unknotting as we walked. I breathed in the clear, sharp air and I was happy. Ruth smiled up at me, I grinned back. No words. We did not need them.

After a while I realized that we were walking along hand in hand, although I could not remember our hands linking, Cormorants were sailing above our heads, catching the breeze in their wings and drifting wherever the gusts took them, calling mournfully. In the distance, I could make out the shapes of fishing boats heading out for the day. I supposed that somebody in. the village should be in a position to offer me a berth to the mainland, but something in me unexpectedly rebelled at the idea. England and the Spanish Civil War seemed like a dream to me now. The sun on my cheeks, the breeze on my neck, the heat of her hand in mine. This was the only reality.

"I don't know how I can properly repay you," I said after a while, and my words were just the vocalized part of a whole string of messages between us, passed in the pressure of our hands and the warmth of our expressions.

"No need," Ruth replied, smiling gently. "Friendship isn't a debt. "

We both stopped walking at the same moment and turned to face one another. We were in a bare area some thirty feet across on the cliff edge. A carved pole had been tuck into the ground in the centre of the clearing, its pointed cap thru ting proudly into the sky. With the crunch of sand under our feet silenced, the soft whisper of the waves flowed in to fill the space. We stood quietly, till with our fingers entwined. The pupils of her eyes were large and deep. I could see my elf reflected in them, and behind me the sky and the cormorants wheeling and swooping.

"We don't know where you came from," she said, the smile fading into seriousness, "and we know you don't want to talk about it. That' all right. You've been hurt and you're still not healed, but as long as you want to stay you're perfectly welcome to, with no need to repay us for anything. There's some in the village who say we shouldn't have anything to do with strangers, but Jethro and l don't agree. You were hurt, and it's our obligation to heal you. We don't know what your plans are, or whether you want to stay on the island or not, but for as long as you want to be with us, our home is yours." Her lips began to curl as she tried to suppress a grin and failed. "So long as you do the cooking and the washing up, clean the hut every day, fetch the food and the water and... "

My hands caught her just underneath her ribs and squeezed.

Ruth squealed, wide eyed in surprise, and writhed as I tickled her. Laughter tingled in the air. Her surprise and her giggles were so natural that [could not help joining in, even as she attempted to escape. Somehow she ended up pressing closer to me. Her body was warm and soft. She smelled of summer. Our laughter grew quieter, grew quiet. I remembered Jethro.

"J think we'd better get going." I said.

Ruth nodded. silent. Our eyes held, then we moved apart and started walking again.

We were both more subdued on the way to the village, but as the first few stone houses appeared along the edges of the path, Ruth began to unbend.

"It's market day today," she confided. "The whole village'll be there, and the ones like Jethro who live further away – nigh on two hundred people. There'll be stuff that's been made, and stuff that's been grown, and stuff that's come from the mainland. We still trade with the mainland folk. Some of them, anyway. There's things like cloth, and rigging for the boats, that we just can't make ourselves, and there's always mainlanders who wouldn't let bad words spoil a bargain."

"Bad words?" I asked. I had already realized that contact between the islanders and the mainlanders was slight, but this was the first time that either Ruth or Jethro had referred to it directly. I supposed that it might make returning to England more difficult, but I was not sure whether to be annoyed or pleased.

"They say we're heathens," she said, turning her face away. "They say we're going to go to Hell."

Houses appeared in huddled twos and threes. We passed a church, dilapidated and empty, and I asked Ruth if there was a priest or a pastor on the island. She glanced oddly at me and shook her head. People with closed, suspicious faces stared at me as we walked past. If I smiled back at them they looked away. There seemed to be a marked similarity between many of the people, as if they were all part of the same extended family. After a while I could pick out characteristics – flat stares, heavy eyebrows, wide faces – that seemed to be common. Many of them seemed to resemble Jethro, or perhaps Jethro resembled them. One or two looked like Ruth. A large woman in mismatched clothes who had fine, downy hair covering her face and hands watched us pass. She had two children with her who gazed up at me with unreadable expressions on their furred faces.

We walked on like this for ten minutes or so, with the number of houses and people around us increasing, until we were in the centre of a bustling crowd in the market square. Brightly coloured stalls were scattered haphazardly around the cobbled area, selling food, clothes, household items, animals and roughly made pieces of furniture. The smell of cooking and tanning drifted over everything. I followed Ruth from stall to stall a she bartered and dickered and promised, all with a smile on her face. I smiled too, but the faces of the islanders turned sour as they glanced at me out of the corners of their eyes.

As I walked I became aware of a small figure flitting through the crowd. Whichever way I turned, it seemed to turn with me. I was being followed. I tried to get a closer look, but the crowd seemed to thicken wherever it moved. I tried to attract Ruth's attention, but she was busy bargaining over a loaf of bread. Leaving her side, I attempted to edge toward the figure, but my progress was suddenly impeded by villagers suddenly too slow or too clumsy' to get out of my way. By the time I got to the spot where I had seen it, leaving a flurry of elbow's and muttered apologies in my wake, it had gone.

I turned to make my way back to Ruth but. as I did so, a sudden eddy in the throng opened up a space across which I caught sight of my pursuer. I was only afforded a momentary glimpse before the crowd moved again, closing the gap, but in that long moment my eyes met her. She had the body of a child, and yet, as she looked over her shoulder at me, her face was baggy and wizened, and her eyes were vacant.

The sights, the sounds and the smells of the market swirled around me as I tried to understand what I had seen. Eventually, when nothing more happened, I turned back to the stalls. Ruth was arguing happily over a box of root vegetables, but as I moved to join her, I caught sight of a stall selling pieces of driftwood carved into animals, faces, and abstract forms. It was the first time that I had seen anything resembling art on the island, and I took a closer look. One particular sculpture caught my eye. It must have weighed a couple of pounds, and took the shape of a curved, slightly fluted, column with a conical cap – a mushroom, perhaps, or something more symbolic. It was a crude piece of work, but it had an undeniable power. It reminded me of the pole in the clearing that Ruth and I had stopped by, up on the cliff.

"How much?" I asked the man on the other side of the stall.

He stared at me for a long moment.

"Not for sale," he said eventually, reaching over and taking it roughly from me. His face was weather-worn and old, the skin cracked and grained like one of his carvings. I guessed him at about fifty.

"I'm a friend of Ruth and Jethro," I said, more to

fill the silence than for any other reason.

"Aye, you'll be the one they salvaged from the sea." He spat on the ground.

His casual manner offended me. "They've been very kind."

"Aye, well they've got good cause."

"What do you mean?"

He smiled. His teeth were tobacco-mottled and rotting. "You'll find out."

A woman with a deeply lined, wary face came over and stood beside him. I smiled at her, but there was no response.

"He's the stranger," she said to the man.

"Excuse me," I said, "but is there somebody with a boat I could talk to?"

"He'll not get off the island," she muttered. "She'll not let him go." .

"Who won't?" I made as if to move around the stall and confront her, but the man put his arm around her shoulders protectively.

"You'd best catch up with your lass," he said. "There's nothing for you here."

I wanted to continue asking him about boats, and who exactly it was that wouldn't let me off the island, but I had noticed that something was wrong with his hand. Trying not to be obvious, I shifted to get a better look, and recoiled, shocked, as I realized that the index finger of his right hand branched into two smaller fingers at the first knuckle.

Ruth was suddenly at my side, with a brittle smile on her face. She took my arm and moved me away.

"They don't like me," I said.

"You're a stranger," she said. "Tobias and Rachel don't like strangers."

"Do any of them?" I asked, looking around at the sea of suspicious faces. ,

"Some of them are reasonable," Ruth responded with a quirk of her lips. "Rachel's husband, Elisha, has no bad feelings for anybody, But then, he's a stranger, like you."

"I thought Rachel was married to Tobias," I said, determined to avoid any future misunderstandings by getting everybody's name and relationship down pat.

Ruth looked confused. "She is."

Now it was my turn to look confused. "But you just said she was married to Elisha."

"She is."

We were both frowning now, unsure of our ground.

"So... hang on a second. Rachel is married to both Tobias and Elisha?"

"Yes... What's wrong?" Ruth looked genuinely puzzled.

"I..."

There was a voice behind me, calling. Ruth smiled over my shoulder and began to wave.

"Sarah!" she yelled. "Sarah!" Her eyes flickered

onto me semi-apologetically. "Sarah's my half-sister." Then she was pushing past me and slipping like a fish through the crowd shouting, "You're looking so well, Sarah. How much longer?"

"A few months yet, the old 'un told me," said Sarah. She was young, about the same age as Ruth, but broader and blond. What I had taken to be puppy fat was, on closer inspection, a pregnant bulge. I tried to move toward them but Ruth was smaller and more used to the crowds than I, and I was swept sideways by a good few feet before I could recover and fight my way through. People stepped aside for me, but not out of kindness. I fielded their hostility with smiles and murmurs of thanks. By the time I got to Ruth and Sarah they were saying good-bye. There was a quick introduction, a flashed smile. and a silent look exchanged between the two of them. Then Sarah was gone, escorted by two young men and an older woman who had been standing silently beside her.

"No doubt she's married to all of them," I said quietly, watching them go. I do not know if I was being facetious or not. Sarah was holding hands with the two men as they walked. The woman trailed behind.

"Of course not," said Ruth. She sounded...not shocked, but some lesser level closer to surprise. "She hasn't had the baby yet."

That halted the conversation for some time.

We walked around the market for a while longer, then I asked Ruth if we could make a move for home. I was tiring, and my leg was beginning to throb.

It seemed to be a shorter walk back. We said little. As we drew nearer to Jethro and the hut, Ruth gestured down at the beach.

"The tides are funny around here," she said suddenly. "Somehow the pebbles get sorted in the water. The sand gets washed up by the hut, and the larger pebbles end up down by the village. The fishermen say that wherever they beach their boats they can tell where they are, just by the size of the pebbles."

"Ruth, how can Rachel be married to two men at once?"

"That's the way it happens," she said.

"Not in other places."

"We're a long way from the mainland." "Why does that matter?"

"It matters."

Silence for a while. The trees lining the path cowered backward from the sea in positions of frozen horror. Years of storms had fixed them into the best shape for survival. Down below us, by the seashore, the hut came into sight. It looked so small. I could not see Jethro anywhere. Beyond it lay the wreck – graceless, like a beached whale.

"And Sarah? My God, Ruth, the girl's not even married yet and she's having a baby."

"What's so wrong about that?"

"She should marry the father."

"She will. Both of them."

My face must have reflected my shock. Ruth stopped and grabbed my arms, trying to make me understand.

"Sarah will get married, just as soon as she's had the baby. As soon as it's been named. What's wrong with that?"

"Married to who?"

"To all of them."

"And what about that woman who was with them?"

"Betty? She's already married to them. She's had four children named already."

"What's so special about naming a baby?"

She frowned, unsure of how serious I was. "You can't have a baby named unless it's whole."

"Whole?"

She was angry now. "Two arms. Two legs. A face. Not deaf or blind. Not dead."

"Don't be an idiot!" I was angry too. She had no right to be furious at my ignorance. "How often does that actually happen?"

Silence. A small voice. "One in every three." Suddenly her face crumpled and she began to cry. I moved forward and took her in my arm. Warm tears dampened my shirt. Jethro's shirt. I took her face in my hands and raised it until Ruth was looking at me with bleary, beautiful, almond-shaped eyes. I leaned forward and kissed the tears away one by one. They tasted of salt.

"Oh God, I think I'm pregnant too," she

whispered into my ear. I moved my head back to look at her. Silent tears still trickled from screwed-up eyes. I kissed her properly this time, long and slow. Her body pressed into mine. Time and identity melted together and it seemed only seconds later that we were naked, although I cannot remember removing her clothes or mine. We fitted together like two perfectly machined engine parts, moving in a regular rhythm. Her face was screwed up tight. The breeze was cool on my back, the sand warm beneath my hands and knees. My body tingled. As she gasped and I cried out I felt her hand tighten on my shoulder, but then her arms slid around my waist as she gazed up into the cloudless blue sky, and I looked up, and Jethro stared down at me. He was smiling, and one of his hands held my shoulder while the other caressed Ruth's face with gentle, loving strokes. He was so pleased for us. God help me, he was so pleased,

I still remember his expression, although it was months ago now. Sarah – Ruth's half-sister – gave birth last week. She married the two men who might have been the father as soon as the baby had been pronounced whole, and named. I was not allowed to attend. Ruth had been tearful, Jethro resolute. The old 'un would not have permitted it, I was told. I had not yet been accepted by the islanders.

I asked who the old 'un was, to dictate their marriages, their lives, their loves? I said that I did not understand how they could let their lives be blighted by one person's word. Ruth started to explain, but Jethro cut her short.

'We should go," he said, and took her arm. She glanced back at me as he opened the door.

"I'm coming," I said, and got up.

"Thomas...no!" The fear in her eyes stopped me cold. "Thomas, I... "

The door closed before she could finish.

I watched from the window as they made their way along the foot of the cliff. Part of me wanted just to lie down and rest, but I knew that I had to follow. Something was sour at the heart of this island, and I cared enough for Ruth – yes, and for Jethro too – that I needed to know what it was.

I left the hut and sprinted along the beach, staying close to the sea, hidden from Ruth and Jethro by the low rolling dunes. By the 'time I caught up with them, they had joined a procession from the village that had Sarah, her baby, and her suitors at its head. Although I only caught glimpses of them as I ran, it seemed to me that there were more people in the procession than I had believed were on the island. Somehow it did not surprise me that they were heading for one of the many caves along the base of the cliff. Under cover of the dunes I managed to run ahead, so that by the time Sarah led the way in to the shadowed opening I was crouched, watching, behind a large clump of sea grass. For the first time I could see the villagers clearly and the sight made me almost sick.

I saw abominations in that procession the like of which I have never seen before, and pray to God I never see again: twins joined at the shoulder, people with enlarged or shrunken heads, a man whose lips were mere ragged fringes surrounding his teeth and who chewed at his fingers as he walked. One by one they entered the cave.

"They still make my stomach turn," said a reedy voice behind me. I looked over my shoulder. A thin man in an overly large sweater was crouching some yards behind me. His grey hair hung in greasy ringlets about his ears but thinned out to the point of baldness above his brow.

"Elisha," he said. "You'll be the other stranger."

"Other?"

"My fishing boat foundered on the rocks twenty years ago now. They still call me 'stranger'."

"You're Rachel's husband," I said, remembering the market and the start of my argument with Ruth.

"Rachel's *other* husband," he reminded me gently, and glanced over at the cave mouth, from which the sounds of distant chanting echoed.

"They only come out for special occasions," he said. "The feeble ones. The crippled ones. The ones who aren't quite right in the head. Only come out for namings and marriages. They're kept apart the rest of the time. The islanders don't like to be reminded."

"Reminded of what?"

He looked at me strangely. "God's judgment."

"What did they do wrong?"

"They married each other. No limit on this island. Marry who you like."

The sound of massed voices raised in song drifted across the sand.

"How did it all start?" I asked. "They can't always have been like this, surely?"

Elisha smiled sadly, and rubbed his nose. "They claim a wise woman came to live amongst them, long time ago now. She'd been persecuted on the mainland, and came here for refuge. They say she could do the most incredible things: tell the future, make potions for lovers, fly through the air. Must have been a forceful personality, by all accounts; after all, her mark is still on the island. She took lots of lovers, and encouraged the islanders to do the same. There were ceremonies in which they would all dance around a pole set in the ground, stark naked, and then take each other like so many animals rutting." He laughed suddenly. "Like I say, she must have been a forceful personality, because they're still doing it. Or perhaps the hexes she cast are still working on the islanders."

"What about... "

"The Church?" He snorted, and spat onto the sand. "The local pastor was driven out according to one story I was told, driven mad according to another. Can't say I'm surprised.'

He fell silent, listening to the singing.

"What happened to this wise woman?" I asked.

"She's still here," Elisha said and nodded toward the cave mouth. "They call her the old 'un."

"Have you seen her?"

Elisha smiled, and looked out to sea.

"Of yes," he said, "I've seen her."

Odd facts and throwaway lines started to meet up in my mind like a child's join-the-dots puzzle.

"That's why the mainlanders won't have any contact with the islanders!"

"They say the islanders are Godless," Elisha confirmed. "One or two whose greed overcomes their piety will trade, but that's on the sly."

"But that means…" My thoughts were racing ahead of my mind now, but I didn't dare articulate those thoughts. Elisha did it for me.

"Oh, they're all related," he said, nodding towards the cave. "There's been no fresh blood for generations now. The island's all one, big, happy family. Didn't you know? Jethro is Ruth's brother."

I felt as if I had become detached from the world I thought I understood. The feel of the sand beneath my feet faded away; the sound of the surf retreated into a faint hissing. I heard a voice ask a question, and it was only when Elisha answered that I realized it had been me who said: "So that was God's punishment? Deformities?"

"That, or barrenness. Couples aren't allowed to marry here until they prove they can bear a normal child. If they can't then they aren't allowed to have any more children. That way the islanders try not to spread the deformities through the population."

He smiled proudly at me. "I'm not saying it's to do with marrying within the family, but all ten of my children are healthy." The smile faded from his face. "Not that it's done any good. It seems like every year there are more freaks and misfits on the island. That's why the old 'un wants you to stay. You're an injection of health into a decaying population."

Elisha's quiet, normal tone had pulled me back from wherever I had floated off to. "They don't kill the children?" I asked.

"No. But they don't like having them around. If it makes my stomach turn, what does it do for them?"

There was silence from the cave, and suddenly the islanders started to emerge, blinking into the daylight, like parishioners leaving church. Sarah and Ruth were last, gossiping and laughing. Jethro held back from the crowd and reached out a hand to Ruth. She took it coyly. I looked within myself for any hatred towards him, but I could find none. If Ruth loved him, how could I not?

"She's a beautiful woman. You're very lucky."

"Am I?" I whispered.

"They'll be heading up to the marriage pole now," he said wistfully. "Sarah'll get married to the two lads, and then they'll all follow the old tradition. They still don't let me join in, being a relative newcomer and all, but I like to watch." He put his hand on my shoulder. "Do you want to come?"

I turned away. After a few moments he muttered, "Suit yourself," and left.

After I was sure that all the villagers had left, I walked across to the cave. The sun was dipping towards the sea, turning the waves to crimson and silhouetting the soaring cormorants. The closer I got, the more familiar it looked.

A few feet past its entrance the cave widened out into a chamber the size of an aeroplane hangar. The last rays of the sun shone through potholes and fissures high in the cliff face and cast thin beams of light across the empty space. Stalactites like folded sheets of dirty lace hung from the high ceiling. As I stepped forward into the main body of the cave I looked down. The floor appeared to drop away before my feet, plunging into shadowed depths where grotesquely twisted stalagmites reached up blindly towards their cousins. I could see no path, no space where the islanders could have congregated. Then, as the stalagmites rippled gently in my vision, I realized that they were too perfect, too close a representation of the stalactites above. I bent and reached forward. For a second my fingers were cold and the cave shook before my eyes, and then my fingers met rock. I let out a breath I did not even realize I had been holding. A thin layer of water covered the floor of the cave, and it was the reflection of the stalactites that had fooled me.

I stepped forward, my feet splashing the water

and causing ripples to spread out, making the illusory stalagmites shimmer like a dream. Ahead of me a large chunk of stone obstinately refused to change. As I got closer I realized how large it was – a chunk of limestone slightly smaller and almost as broad as I was. It was the only stalagmite that rose from the floor of the cave. The centuries-old dripping of water from the roof of the cave had weathered it into complex patterns, and constant trickle had etched deep folds into its body. In the half-light of sunset it could almost be taken for a cowled figure with folded arms. The stone on a level with my eyes had even been weathered into feature – rounded approximations to the human face, like the gargoyles poised around old churches, waiting for the souls of the dead.

Like an old woman with cruel, lined features.

If there ever had been a wise woman living in the village then she was long dead, her memory kept alive by the islanders and by the accidental similarity of a chunk of stone. I turned to go.

"Thomassss..."

I spun round. Water splashed around my feet. Nothing moved.

"Thomassss..."

"Who's there?" I shouted. "Jethro? Ruth?"

"Join ussss..."

The wind whistling through fissures in the rock? The half-heard trickle of far-off water? The noise echoed in the shadows, fainter and fainter, until it was gone. Nothing moved and nothing spoke as I stalked out of the cave.

*   *   *

I spend a lot of time on the beach now. I have my favourite spot, nestled between two steep-banked and dunes and protected from the wind and the wind-borne sea spray. From it I can see the wide sweep of the bay and the white caps to the waves that might be the foam as they curl and break, or the cormorants riding them and diving for food. I often come here to sit, remembering the life I used to have, watching the fishing boats heading out for the day and wishing I had the courage to be on one of them.

The wreck of the old De Havilland DH16 is overgrown now. Grasses and weeds have sprouted unchecked through and around it, tough sea grasses that can adapt to any conditions and survive anywhere. The cormorants seem quite happy. I got angry with them last week and chased down the shingle towards them, arms flapping hysterically, driving them away if only for a moment. Flushed with my success I sat on one of the charred struts. The structure creaked under me. As I adjusted my position, my foot brushed an object, half buried in the shingle. I bent to pick it up. It was a book, old and faded now, pages made brittle by the sea. The leather cover cracked as I opened it up. A tiny puff of dust bled onto my palm. The ink had faded, of course, but I still remembered the words I had written on the flyleaf all those years ago.

Thomas Paul Jerome. Flight logbook. August 1933.

With a strong overarm case I managed to hurl it a few yards closed to the English coast. A cormorant was ducking for food near to where it sank. The bird looked up at me disdainfully, then returned to its feeding. I watched it for a while. Food, and the sea, and the wreck – these were its world. The island was mine. The cormorants could fly away to the mainland, or further if they wished, but habit bound them here. I was tied by love, and I could not, would not, leave.

AS NEAR TO FLAME AS LUST TO SMOKE

I am no viper, yet I feed,
On mother's flesh which did me breed;
I sought a husband, in which labour,
I found that kindness in a father.
He's father, son and husband mild.
I mother. wife, and yet his child.
How they may be, and yet in two,
As you will be, resolve it you.

The expanding ball of flame carried the fragile chariot up with it, tumbling it in mid-air and flinging its passengers off like a bucking stallion. A wheel came loose and spun lazily away from the twisted mass of metal while burning leather thongs and fragments of wood rained down upon the plain, trailing ribbons of smoke behind them.

Only moments before, Lord Thaliard had watched as a cloud of dust approached the low foothills where he was camped. The cloud had soon resolved itself into a group of chariots, one leading the others by several hundred yards. In its prow King Antiochus the Third, Son of Seleucus and undisputed King of Syria, had been whipping his horses onward, his robes billowing in the wind and the sun glinting on the jewels of his crown. The chariots of his elite guards had been

Left hundreds of yards behind as the king showed off his legendary horsemanship, head thrown back and laughing as he rode. Behind him, a veiled figure wound one hand around his waist. Her dark hair streamed in the wind of the chariot's frantic passage, and Thaliard's heart beat faster as he recognized Thea, Antiochus's daughter.

For a moment, as he stood there on the hillside watching the chariots approach, Thaliard had wondered how he was going to explain the failure of his mission. Pericles, Prince of Tyre, still lived. Antiochus would not be pleased. And that meant Thea would not be pleased.

And then the fire came, erupting from the midst of the dust, lifting the chariot up toward the heavens like an offering to the Gods.

Thaliard watched, horrified, as Antiochus arid Thea fell screaming from the wreckage. The King thrashed his arms and legs wildly as he plummeted, while Thea's robes and hair were an eye-searing inferno of flame. Thaliard could not turn away: his fingernails dug into the palms of his hands and his scalp seemed to crawl as they both hit the ground and bounced, coming to rest near the dismembered bodies of their horses. Even at that distance Thaliard could see that their bodies were bent double and twisted. Greasy smoke rose from Thea's blackened remains.

Fragments of chariot continued to rain down on them for several moments longer.

"Great Rimmon protect us," Eucaerus, Thaliard's most trusted lieutenant, whispered from beside him. His face was ashen, the scar he had gained during his time as a spy in Greece livid against his skin. The flames gilded his greying hair with scarlet. "The wrath of the Gods has fallen upon him for his sins!"

"What sins?" Thaliard snapped.

"I meant – " Eucaerus stopped. Thaliard would have turned to. look at him, but his attention was distracted by what was happening down on the plain, where Antiochus's guards had caught up with the scattered wreckage. They stayed in their chariots, keeping their distance from the body of their king and gazing fearfully up to the encampment on the hillside. They were waiting for direction, and Thaliard knew it was him they were looking to. He had been Antiochus's favourite, after all; his trusted right hand.

"Bring the bodies here," he said without turning, "And send a messenger to Antioch with the news." He heard Eucaerus turn to leave, and added, "And have the priesthood sacrifice three goats to Rimmon to ease the path of their souls."

Without moving from his position, he watched as the bodies – or what was left of them – were carefully gathered up in silken sheets and carried away with fear and reverence. Once the plain was deserted Thaliard turned his back on it and strode toward the camp. He had left it in the hills while he undertook his mission in Tyre. When he had arrived back, unsuccessful, he. had dispatched Eucaerus to Antioch as a messenger, expecting to be summoned. immediately back to court, but Eucaerus had returned to say that the king and his daughter would arrive within the hour. The largest tent had been immediately set aside for a feast. Now it acted as a temporary resting place for their bodies.

Entering, Thaliard dismissed the soldiers and priests. Grypus, High Priest of the House of Rimmon, approached him as the rest left. His ornate robes, scarlet embroidered with gold thread, brushed the: ground as he walked. "A tragedy." he murmured, his voice stern and deep. "There must be mourning across the land."

"It will be so ordered," Thaliard said. Grypus hesitated for a moment, and Thaliard turned to meet his questioning gaze. "Yes?"

"It would be... unfortunate... if the apotheosis of King Antiochus were to lead to a struggle for power in the land. A firm hand is required."

"Apotheosis?"

Grypus shrugged. "The Gods are powerful and capricious. What would be more natural than for them to recognise those same qualities in Antiochus and wish for him to become one of them?"

"And Thea?"

Grypus's face twisted, as if he bad bitten into something sour. "King Antiochus will require a… companion in heaven."

"One might have expected the Gods to provide

such a man as him with a woman who could fulfil his more physical desires," Thaliard snapped, suppressing a sudden rush of grief and anger, "rather than take his daughter from our midst to serve his needs,"

"Perhaps," Grypus said quietly, "the Gods know more than we do."

Ignoring Grypus's cryptic words, Thaliard thought for a moment. The priest was a practical man. His explanation was a convenient one., and it would calm the populace more than the suggestion that the Gods had been displeased with Antiochus's actions. Gazing into Grypus's eyes he could tell that the priest believed it as little as he did. "Very well," he said, "Antiochus is now with the Gods. What of Syria?

"There are… factions… who might wish to take the throne themselves."

"Antiochus's only son died years ago," Thaliard said quietly, "and three of his daughters ate already married to rulers of other lands who have no interest in Syria. Thea, of course, isn't married. The riddle has always prevented that."

"There are others," Grypus said. "There are always others. His brother, Philopator, was named co-regent during his campaigns in India. Philopator is an ambitious man."

"So am I." Thaliard looked away. "I appreciate your honesty. Don't worry: Rimmon will decide."

When Grypus had followed the rest of the priests and servants out of the tent, Thaliard approached the first of the two shrouded tables that were now acting as biers, and carefully lifted the sodden material.

The sour smell of blood was nothing new to him. He was an assassin and a soldier. He bad bathed in blood, waded through it, seen it stream from bodies like wine pouring from a ripped wineskin. Blood did not frighten him. But this…

In death, as in life, King Antiochus had demanded more than any other man. One death was not enough for him, and so he had to have three. His body had been rent as if by the cuts of a thousand knives, then his skin scorched and cracked by the mystical fire that had destroyed his chariot, and then he had been broken by the fall so that his limbs were twisted into grotesque shapes. His eyes, mercifully, were closed, but his lip. were still curved into the grin Thaliard had seen on his face just before the fire had blossomed around him.

"My king," Thaliard murmured softly, "Rimmon grant me the wisdom and the power to rule as mercifully and justly as you have done."

Bending forward, he gently kissed Antiochus upon his bloody lips, then pulled the material back to cover his face.

He hesitated before approaching the second table. The material covering Thea's body was greasy and soot-stained rather than bloodied, and the stench of cooked meat that rose from it was almost overpowering. Whatever power had visited Antiochus, it had dwelled longer with his daughter.

That soft, peach-fuzzed skin. Those pale blue eyes. The knowing half-smile on those lips…

He reached out and pulled the sheet off before he could change his mind.

Thea's body looked more like a carcass cooked for a banquet than it did a woman. Her pale, smooth skin was now brown. blackened in places, and slick with fat; her body was shrunken and, the tendons of her arms and neck stood out dearly. Fragments of burned silk were embossed on her skin. Her face – Great Rimmon: her face was just a charred shape, bereft of features and coated with half-melted clumps of hair. Thaliard felt his stomach heave and took a deep breath, quelling it. This was not the time. Later, perhaps, in the privacy of his own tent, but not now, not here, where so many invisible eyes would be watching him, weighing his bearing and his actions.

Before he had left for Tyre, he had told her how much he loved her. She had laughed, and said that he had to solve her father's riddle first like everyone else. He had taken his life into his hands then and kissed her, roughly, pinning her arms behind her back, but she hadn't resisted. As he had left her, Thaliard had smiled to himself, expecting some coaching on the answer to the riddle when it came time for him to answer it. He would need the coaching: failure to answer the riddle didn't just mean failure to win Thea's hand... it meant a painful and ignominious death.

But the death hadn't been his.

He started to cast the sheet back over her remains, and paused.

Something was wrong. There was a smell: sweet and heavy on the air. A smell that reminded him of the Temple of Rimmon. He bent closer to the body and, ignoring as best he could the smell of cooked meat, he sniffed.

It was stronger now: the same smell as the oil that they burned in the temple on ceremonial days. Frankincense, the priests called it. Had the bodies been prepared for burial already? There hadn't been time, he was sure of it. Perhaps Thea had used something similar as a perfume, or in her bath; but no, the smell was far too strong, Before the fire it would have been overpowering, and Thea had always disdained excess.

Something was amiss. He could feel it tugging at his mind.

Frankincense burned easily, he had seen that in the temple, and Thea's body was burned to a far greater extent than her father's. Heaven-sent fire was one thing... the Gods could not be questioned or brought to account for the things they did... but this was a different matter. The Gods did not need human help with their fiery thunderbolts.

He straightened up, keeping his face expressionless for the benefit of whatever observers were hidden behind the walls of the tent. Quickly, he crossed back to the bier upon which Antiochus lay and pulled the sheet away. It was the king, there could be no doubt about that, bur when Thaliard looked at his face he did not see a grin of superiority any more: be saw a grimace of fear. A knowledge of impending death.

Thaliard bent even closer and sniffed, but could smell no frankincense. That was strange: why should Thea, but not her father, be covered in the oil? That was the reason her body was more burned than his, but it didn't make any sense.

Oil. Oil that the priests used. Oil that caught fire easily and could not be put out. "Powerful and capricious", Grypus had said, and Grypus was the High Priest. Had there been a power struggle of some sort between Temple and State that Thaliard had been unaware of? Had *Grypus,* rather than the Gods he served, caused Antiochus's death?

How could he? Frankincense burned, but not by itself. It had to be set alight by something, and there had been no sign that either Antiochus or Thea had done so in the chariot. Letting the sheet fall, Thaliard turned and strode out of the room.

Gods could not be questioned. But men could.

Eucaerus's tent was his first destination. The two guards came to attention with a clank of armour as Thaliard approached. By the time he entered the tent, his lieutenant was gazing expectantly at the opening. Eucaerus had been removing his breastplate, and something about his position, and the swaying material that separated the front of the tent from the sleeping quarters at the back, told Thaliard that he had not been alone.

"My Lord?" His voice still held a trace of a Greek accent. He had developed it during the years he had lived there and spied on the Greeks for Antiochus.

"Eucaerus, I need your assistance. When you rode to Antioch, did you see Thea?"

"I did, my Lord."

"And how did she seem to you?"

He smiled, and his lined face seemed to soften slightly. "She seemed even more beautiful than I remembered, my Lord."

"Was she wearing perfume?"

Eucaerus frowned. "My Lord?"

"Was Thea wearing perfume?"

"Not that I could detect, my Lord," Eucaerus replied

Thaliard scowled. "And how was Antiochus?"

"As dynamic and forceful as ever."

"Neither of them were worried? Concerned? Fearful?"

Eucaerus shook his head. "No, my Lord."

"And what of Antiochus's brother, Philopator? Did you see him?"

"I understand he is away from. Antioch at the moment."

The suspicion of Grypus that Thaliard had been nurturing suddenly shifted toward Philopator. How convenient that he was absent, just when his brother had been killed. Philopator's brief reign as regent during Antiochus's campaign in India had been lax, and his distraction had allowed the economy to slide. Antiochus had been forced to. take strict measures to recover the country's prosperity upon his return. Was be now building an army? Was he preparing to take the throne of Syria for himself?

Philopator or Grypus. Either way, his course was clear. He bad to get back to the court and protect the country.

"Eucaerus, prepare to strike camp. We must return to Antioch as soon as possible."

"As my lord instructs."

Outside the tent the sun was just touching the horizon, and the sky was layered with crimson and purple clouds. Thaliard tried to lose himself in the sight, to let himself melt into the landscape and still the ceaseless circling of his thoughts, but it was no use. All he saw when he looked at the sunset was the blossoming fire on the plain.

His thoughts ran wildly, like a chariot in the hands of an inexperienced driver. What had caused the ball of fire? More puzzling still: why bad it been necessary for Thea's body to be more badly burned than her father's? The grimace on his face, whether pain or pleasure, could still be seen, but Thea's features were unrecognizable.

Unrecognizable. Thaliard held the word in his mind, turning it like a dark jewel, examining it for flaws. Unrecognizable. Almost as if by design...

His arrival at his own tent broke his chain of thoughts. There were four guards in front of it rather than the usual two, and their breastplates were freshly polished. He seemed to be slipping into the role of king without conscious effort, Those around him treated. him as king, he gave orders like a king, what was a coronation but a validation of something indefinable that had already occurred?

There was someone waiting for him in his tent: a bulky figure wearing a tunic of fine cloth and a purple cloak.

"Lord Philopator!" Thaliard kneeled. The soldiers outside - how could he have been so arrogant? They weren't for him at all, they were Philopator's personal bodyguards.

"Lord Thaliard - please, rise." Philopator waved a vague hand, and Thaliard stood.

"You honour my humble camp with – "

"Let us save time by abandoning the formalities: Philopator said.

Thaliard glanced up. Philopator's fleshy lips were curled into a half-smile but Thaliard sensed another expression lurking behind his face, one he could not quite make out. "I had travelled to Antioch to see my brother when I heard he had ridden out to greet you. I followed, only to find..." His hand waved toward the plain. "I could ask what your plans are, Thaliard, but I suspect I might not believe your answer. The penalties of having been involved in too many court intrigues: everything becomes intrigue after a while and all answers are assumed to be lies. Equally, you could ask me my plans, but you have no reason to believe my answer any more than I would believe yours."

"Then where does that leave us?" Thaliard asked.

Philopator shrugged. "For what it is worth, let me volunteer some information. You may choose to believe it or not." He looked away, toward where the plain lay beyond the confines of the tent. "I have no desire to rule Syria. I tried it once, when Antiochus was campaigning in India, and I found I had no talent for it. Being a regent sapped my time and energy for no reward that I could not obtain by other means. And besides - the risks are too great for my liking." He turned back, and the hidden expression had broken through his half-smile; an earnest, almost begging look. "Should you wish to become king, Thaliard, I will not stand in your way. More than that: I will pledge myself to you."

Thaliard felt a hysterical laugh bubbling up within his breast, and suppressed it ruthlessly. The future of Syria could well rest upon what was said in this tent. "Events are moving too fast for us, Lord Philopator. We should discuss this later when…" He meant to say, "When the blood on King Antiochus's body isn't still wet," but he just trailed off instead…

Philopator nodded. "My offer stands for as long as it takes you; to make a decision." The half-smile returned to his lips. "If I return to Antioch, would you trust me not to take the throne, before you arrive?"

Thaliard shrugged slightly, as Philopator had done earlier. "I haven't said it matters to me if you do."

"Of course not," Philopator said. He turned to leave, but Thaliard reached a hand out to stop him.

"You said that the risks of being king were too great for your liking. What did you mean?"

"You're an assassin, Lord Thaliard. You should know." Thaliard turned to look Philopator in the eye; and what he saw was his real expression - not the half-smile, not the earnest begging, but fear. Raw fear.

"I didn't kill King Antiochus," Thaliard whispered.

"Of course not," Philopator said again.

"How could I? That fire - how could any human agency cause it?"

"That presents no great mystery," Philopator shrugged. "Greek Fire, they call it. "The Greeks aren't telling what it is made of but it burns like the very flames of hell and it cannot be put out, not by water anyway. My brother sent many spies to Greece to try and discover what it was, but they came back with. very little information - or so he said. It's a substance like wax that they keep beneath oil, in vases. When they take it out into air it ignites immediately. Or so I have heard." He smiled his little half-smile. "I have never been to Greece."

Like sunrise across a previously unseen landscape, Thaliard suddenly became aware of something so obvious that he could not see bow he could have missed it. "No," he murmured, "but I know someone who has." He rushed out of his tent, past the doubled set of guards, leaving Philopator standing open-mouthed. By the time he was half-way to Eucaerus's. tent he knew what he would find. Eucaerus's guards tried to stop him, but he pushed past them and threw the flap open. He wasn't surprised to see that his lieutenant was gone. Turning, he ran back towards his own tent. Philopator was just leaving, and Thaliard almost knocked him off his feet.

"Lord Thaliard, what – ?"

"No time." Thaliard glanced around. Rough woven rugs covered the floor, along with more comfortable silk cushions. It would take him too long to search them all. There bad to be another way.

He kicked a cushion out of the way in frustration. He didn't know how long he bad, but if he was right then it could only be a matter of minutes. The cushion sailed through the air and hit a pile in one corner of the tent. They scattered, revealing a stretch of woven flooring that seemed darker than the rest.

Thaliard strode over to the corner and bent down to touch the flooring. His fingers came away sticky. Oil. He knocked the rest of the cushions away to reveal a rough clay vase. It sat in a puddle of oil that was leaking from a small hole in its base. Traces of tallow around the hole indicated to Thaliard that neither the hole nor the leakage were an accident.

The oil only just covered a large, irregular block of wax inside the vase. Another few minutes and the wax would have been exposed to the air. Quickly he scraped the remnants of the tallow back across the hole in its base, sealing the oil in.

Straightening, Thaliard looked at Philopator's sweating face. He still wasn't sure. The frankincense pointed to Grypus and the Greek Fire to the vanished Eucaerus, but the vase could have been hidden in his tent by Philopator. He had to narrow it down.

"My Lord," he snapped, "your life is in danger. It is imperative that you stay in this camp tonight and let my forces guard you."

Philopator shrugged. "Very well, Thaliard, if you think it wise."

"This tent is the finest one I have. I insist you rest here for the night. I will sleep elsewhere."

"Whatever you suggest."

Thaliard took a few steps away from the vase and towards the flap of the tent. Philopator's gaze followed him – bewildered but not panicked – and didn't flicker once toward the vase in its puddle of oil.

That settled it. Philopator knew nothing of the vase or its contents. A crimson wave of fury swept over Thaliard. Picking up the vase he moved toward the tent flap, being careful not to slosh the oil inside too much. He didn't know how much – or how little – exposure to air the substance within required before it ignited.

"Thaliard, I don"t understand!" Philopator's

plaintive voice said from inside the tent.

Knowing he had to get rid of the vase as soon as possible, he rushed downhill toward the edges of the camp. The sky was the colour of an old bruise, and the horses were whinnying, as if they smelled something on the wind. A stone turned under his foot and he almost dropped the vase. Oil spilled over his hand, sticky and warm.

Too warm!

He glanced over his shoulder. The camp was clustered behind him; the horses directly ahead, pastured on the gradual slope at the base of the hill. If he threw the vase now the camp would be safe, but it might fall among the horses, and they were worth more to Syria than his soldiers were. He took a deep breath, then jogged on. Once he got beyond the horses he could throw it down onto the plain with impunity.

If he got beyond the horses.

Voices made him hesitate. Two figures were buckling horses to a chariot on the pasture to one side of the path. Distracted, his foot turned on a turned on a stone and again the vase almost fell from his grasp. The clatter of pebbles attracted the attention of the figures, and the largest of them turned. In the meagre light of the fast-fading sky, Thaliard could just make out the features of his most trusted lieutenant.

"Eucaerus!" he shouted, "Stop where you are!"

"Don't try to interfere," Eucaerus shouted. "We're not trying to take the throne. We just want a life for ourselves. A peaceful life." Thaliard looked toward the second, smaller, figure. He couldn't see her face, but he knew who she was. Who she had to be. "Why, Thea?" he asked simply.

She turned, and her face was just a shadow. "Because you could never have let me go, Thaliard," she said. "Because you had to believe I was dead before you would stop looking for me, and Eucaerus and I could find happiness together."

"Thea, I – "

"You what?" she interrupted. "You loved me? Like my father loved me, Thaliard?"

The confrontation seemed to have taken a sudden turn into unfamiliar territory. "He was your father," Thaliard said, frowning, "of course he loved you. That's no reason to kill him."

"You don't understand," she said quietly. "Nobody understands. It was the answer to the riddle. It was in plain sight, right in front of the world, and my father enjoyed the fact that only he and I ever knew. Another secret we shared."

Thaliard felt a sudden, sick realization weighing heavily in his heart.

Remembering Grypus's words, he wondered how many other people had guessed. "What about Pericles?" he asked.

"Pericles was the only other person ever to solve the riddle, so my father sent you to kill him."

"I failed."

"It doesn't matter." Thaliard could see the glint of tears on her cheeks. "I had grown accustomed to the… to the things my father and I did… the things he forced me to do… but seeing the contempt on Pericles's face when he understood the answer to the riddle made me suddenly wake up and realize what I had become… what had been done to me, Pericles has gone, and it doesn't matter whether he is alive or dead – I've had my revenge on Antiochus now. I made him ride in that chariot, strapped to the reins with the means of his death in a vase between his feet, Eucaerus helped me – he and the few members of my father's guard who were more loyal to Eucaerus than to him. And I almost had my revenge on you, for wanting to do the same to me as my father did. Make me an object. Own me."

"An object? Like the slave – I presume it was a slave – you drenched in frankincense and put on the chariot in your place? Did she deserve what happened to her, just because she had the same build and the same colour hair as you?"

Thea shrugged. "That's what slaves are for: to serve, and to give their lives if we need them."

Thaliard turned back to his lieutenant. His friend. "Don't you see what she's doing, Eucaerus? She's just using you because of your popularity with the guards, and your knowledge of Greek Fire. What was it all for? She's replaced her father with you: a man the same age as he was. How long will you last after you've ceased being useful?"

Eucaerus snarled and took a step toward Thaliard. Thaliard braced himself, but Thea laid a hand on Eucaerus's arm. "Leave him," she said, "he's not important."

That, more than anything, was what cut Thaliard, Nott he betrayal by the lieutenant he trusted, not the betrayal by the woman he had loved, but the casual dismissal.

Eucaerus nodded, and vaulted into the back of the chariot. Extending a hand to Thea, he pulled her up. He glanced back at Thaliard and said: "Don't try to follow us. We have more of the Greek Fire, and we're not afraid to throw it out of the chariot behind us if we're chased."

He flicked the reins. The horses trotted off, and he flicked the reins again to speed them up. Thea slid an arm around his waist to steady herself. Turning, she waved sardonically at Thaliard.

As if he were in a trance, Thaliard lifted his hand to wave back. And realized he was still holding the oil-filled vase.

The chariot speeded up as the gradual slope of the hill gave way to· the level plain, and Eucaerus forced the horses to a gallop. Thaliard swung the vase behind his back. The hot oil spilled across his fingers, burning them. The weight of the vase dragged his arm forward, and he added his strength to it, boosting it higher. As it reached the: top of its arc he could see the silvery meniscus of the oil, with the peak of the wax beneath emerging from it like an island from the sea. He let go, and watched a curious lack of feeling as the vase flew up, tumbling and spilling its oil, before falling toward the retreating chariot and hitting it just behind where Thea was standing.

The oil splashed silver against the night, and for a moment Thaliard could see the dark mass of the wax splatter against her legs.

The expanding ball of flame carried the fragile chariot up with it, tumbling it in mid-air and flinging its passengers off like a bucking stallion. A wheel came loose and spun lazily away from the twisted mass of metal while burning leather thongs and fragments of wood rained down upon the plain, trailing ribbons of smoke behind them.

Thaliard took a deep breath as the remains of the chariot, the horses, Eucaerus and Thea rained down around him. "As your king," he murmured, "I condemn you as traitors, regicides and murderers, and I sentence you to death."

He turned and began the long walk back to his tent, already planning an explanation for the priests to pass on to the people.

To *his* people.

THE GAZE OF THE FALCON

April 4th 1594

Far above his head a falcon hovered like a scrap of black rag on the wings of the wind, the brass bells around its leg signalling its location to its master. What he had sensed had been its finely focused predator's gaze as it scanned him and decided whether or not he counted as prey. As he watched, it folded its wings and plummeted through the air, vanishing behind the line of the forest, and the sensation of being watched vanished with it.

There was such a thing as having senses that were too finely honed.

Chuckling to himself, he walked on, through the rose bushes that the earl's gardeners were training and clipping into a maze. It would be many years before the maze was high enough to shield its design from the eyes of its walkers, but the earl was a man who thought ahead.

As he turned the corner of the house, Shakespeare caught sight of one of the earl's gardeners bending low over a mass of silvery leaves. The mingled smells of sage, lavender and mint made his nose twitch and his stomach rumble. "How goes it?" he asked as he approached.

"Back-breaking work, young master," the

gardener sighed as, he straightened. His wispy white hair blew around his eyes. and he reached up to brush it away with a hand that was as gnarled and as brown as a tree root. "But I've spent my life in this garden, I have, in the service of the earl and of his father before him, God rest his soul, and I wouldn't have it any other way!"

Shakespeare nodded. "Now it is the spring, the weeds are shallow-rooted," he said. "Suffer them now and they'll overgrow the, garden and choke the herbs."

"That's true enough." He gestured at a pile of weeds on the path beside him. "Although life would be simpler if we kept the weeds and pulled up the herbs, they grow that fast," He held his hand, palm out toward Shakespeare. The skin was blistered and red. "Nettle-rash, young master. Dock leaves help take the sting out, but there's' a precious sight more nettles in these beds than there are dock leaves."

His mouth half-way open to make some rejoinder, Shakespeare suddenly noticed a patch of brown fur, half-hidden by the, sage bushes. Bending, he pushed the stems aside. The stench of maggoty meat swamped the smell of the herbs, making his gorge rise.

Lying on the ground beneath the bush was a rabbit, about the size of Shakespeare's hand. The fur around its muzzle was stained black, and parallel gashes marked its back. Its eyes had already decayed back into sticky sockets.

Involuntarily, Shakespeare's gaze flicked

upwards to the clear blue of the morning sky. "Hunting must be good around here," he said, "if the earl's falcons can afford to leave their discarded kills lying around for days on end."

"Aye, young master," the gardener said, hut there was a note of uncertainty in his voice. "Yet that creature wasn't there an hour ago, I swear it."

Shakespeare straightened up, frowning. "From the smell of it that animal has been dead for three or four days. Falcons don't pick up carcasses and throw them down willy-nilly. They only catch live prey."

"I know." The gardener shook his head. "I know. But look at the marks of the claws in its back."

For a moment he couldn't see what the gardener was referring to, and then a shiver ran through him as he noticed.

The gashes where the falcon's claws had ripped into the rabbit were filled with fresh blood, coagulating into purplish clots around the edges.

Shakespeare stared at the rabbit for a few moments more, at the bright red blood on its back and the sunken sockets of its eyes, and then walked away rapidly, his empty stomach suddenly burning with acid. He could feel the gardener's gaze on the back of his neck, prickling like that of the falcon, but he didn't turn back. He did not understand what he had seen, but there had to be an explanation. Everything had an explanation.

He kept walking, his breath steaming in the chilly

morning air, until the gardener was lost around the corner of the house.

After a while Shakespeare thought he could hear the sound of raised voices out in the depths of the forest. He turned his path toward the front of the house, and as he approached the main doors a small group of horsemen and accompanying hounds broke from the trees and cantered toward him. Most of them had hooded bastardes or sakers resting on their outstretched arms, their leather jesses preventing them from flying off. One of the horsemen was riding close beside another, supporting him in the saddle. Shakespeare halted and watched them approach, concern blossoming in his breast.

"My lord!" he cried as the identity of the supported horseman became clear. "What has befallen you?"

"My brother has been taken ill," said William Stanley from his position supporting the Earl. He was burlier than his brother, and concern furrowed his staunch, honest face.

"A pox on that," snapped Ferdinando Stanley, now the Fifth Earl of Derby, but still Lord Strange in Shakespeare's mind. He Was ashen faced, and there were traces of dark vomit staining his jerkin. "I should have - " He paused and bit his lip. "I should have known better than to hunt on an empty stomach. A cramp, that's all."

"No doubt, my lord," another man said. He

supported a bastarde and the earl's own falcon on his gauntletted forearm. "But the sooner we get you to bed and a doctor attending you the better. Especially…" He paused, and Shakespeare noticed a guarded look passing between some of the hunters. "Especially considering how worried Lady Alice will be," he finished weakly.

Shakespeare helped support the earl while William Stanley dismounted. Ferdinando Stanley leaned closer and murmured, "My apologies for this inconvenience, Will. We will have to talk about the new season's plays and the disposition of the Company at some later time."

"I am at your lordship's disposal," Shakespeare murmured.

"It was a fine hunt – a damn fine hunt. Have you ever gone falconing, Will?"

"Never, my lord _ although. I do know a falcon from a heronshaw."

William Stanley draped the earl's arm around his shoulders, and together he and Shakespeare manhandled the earl into the house. The servants flapped around helplessly like a flock of rooks, but together the two men half aided and half dragged the earl to his bedroom where the beautiful and regal Lady Alice shooed them from the room.

Ferdinando Stanley, Fifth Earl of Derby, formerly Lord Strange, died twelve days later.

April 16th 1594

Shakespeare saw the earl twice more, both times on the very day he died. The sharp, sweet smell of decay lay over everything and, as he was ushered into the darkened bedroom, Shakespeare had to quell his churning stomach.

The earl was almost unrecognizable. His skin was blistered and bloody, his beard caked with bile and the bony edges of his skull showed beneath the thin sheet of his skin, but his eyes were alert. He watched as Shakespeare approached the bed.

Doctor Case moved from the bed to intercept him. He held a clove-studded orange beneath his nose. "God will embrace the earl to His bosom before the day is out," he said quietly. "Knowing this, he asked to see you."

"Has he -?"

Case shook his heavy head. "He has kept nothing down since the hunt. Not solids, not liquids, nothing. We have bled him and purged him, we have tried him with poultices and with tinctures, we have given him bezoar, pearls dissolved in wine and the heart and liver of a viper, but to no end. He sinks lower, minute by minute."

Fighting his way through the miasma of putrefaction, Shakespeare came to the edge of the bed and stared down at the face of the man he had loved as his patron. Gratefully he accepted the handkerchief that was pressed into his fist by one of the other physicians. Holding it up to his face, he breathed deeply of the lavender scent.

The earl's lips moved. The dry skin cracked as Shakespeare watched, and a clear liquid seeped out and down his chin. "Leave us," he breathed. His breath stank like a draft from the very mouth of hell.

Obediently and, Shakespeare sensed, with some relief, the physicians withdrew to the open window.

"Will: as you love me, you must help me."

Shakespeare opened his mouth to frame a reassuring reply, but Ferdinando Stanley spoke again.

"I know I am beyond any mortal help now," he whispered, his voice as soft as the wind in the trees, "but listen to me. This was no accident. I have been poisoned."

"Murder most foul!" Shakespeare murmured.

"Listen closely, Will, for only you and my brother will know of this. I wrote to William Cecil before I left London, having learned of a conspiracy to murder the queen and replace her with a Catholic monarch. Kit Marlowe discovered something of the plot last year, and warned me of it before he was done to death."

"Why warn *you*?" Shakespeare asked, keeping his voice low so that the group by the window did not overhear him. Why not warn William Cecil?"

The earl's mouth stretched into a thin parody of a smile, sending fresh rivulets of fluid trickling down his cheeks. "Because the secretary of state would immediately have imprisoned my father and myself as chief suspects: Kit knew we were not involved, and wished to protect us."

Shakespeare nodded slowly. It made a horrible kind of sense. Henry, Fourth Earl of Derby, had been rumoured to have been a closet recusant and Catholic sympathizer, and as the great-nephew of Henry VII he would have had a good claim on the throne of England, had Elizabeth died. "And what of your father's death?" he asked. "Has this matter any bearing on that?"

Ferdinando Stanley blinked slowly: probably the closest he could come to nodding. "I believe he was approached by the plotters and sounded out as figurehead for their schemes. He would have refused: he loved the queen, as I do. Rather than have their plot exposed, they killed him."

"And how do you know all this?" Shakespeare asked, already knowing the answer.

"Because they approached me last month," the earl whispered.

"And you refused them?" Shakespeare asked urgently.

"I did," Stanley sighed. "I love the queen, and would not see her come to harm." He laughed suddenly: a dry, racking sound that convulsed his body. "Often did I tell her that I would give my life for her. Now it looks as if I have!"

"You fear you have been poisoned by these papist plotters?"

"As with my father before me, they fear exposure now that they know where my sympathies lie."

Shakespeare leaned closer, daring the rancid odours of Stanley's body. "Who are they? What are their names? You know I will not rest until I bring them to justice."

"Richard Hesketh, Will Houghton, John Gatside. My brother William has the list, Talk to him. I would ask him to avenge me, but he knows little of intrigue. I know you have worked for Walsingham in the past as an agent of government: you have experience in these things. For the love you bear me... see my murderer to the gallows."

A movement to one side made Shakespeare look up. Doctor Case was approaching the bed, his face wrinkling as he moved away from the fresh air by the window. He held the clove-encrusted orange to his nose and talked around it. "Master Shakespeare, I pray you do not tire the earl. He will need all his strength for the trial ahead."

"I am dying, sawbones," Stanley snapped with something like his old fire, "Let me at least say my piece before I go."

Case retreated with remarkable speed to where the group of physicians were talking, heads together. Shakespeare gazed at them for a long moment, not actually seeing them but casting over in his mind what the earl had said. Something about the whole affair tugged at the back of his mind. Like the gaze of the falcon twelve days ago, he was bothered by something but could not pinpoint its location.

'If you knew that this Hesketh and his minions would try to do you harm," he mused, "then what precautions did you take against their plotting?"

"You saw the group that went a-hunting with me - all trusted men, and all armed. I have travelled nowhere without them. And my food has an been tasted by my servants and my brother before I ate it for months now - I watched them do so." He grimaced. and the sight was so much like the bare grin of a skull that Shakespeare had to look away. "I am not a cowardly man, Will, you of all people know that, but I was determined to live to see their traitorous heads on Tower Bridge. And yet… And yet they found a way to kill me. Had I had not all the charms and amulets that Doctor Dee could provide, I would almost believe it to be witchcraft." His stick-thin arm moved up his chest. His hand, like a bundle of twigs, grasped feebly for something beneath the coverlet. "Look," he said, holding a brown object suspended on a length of silk around his neck out to Shakespeare. "A spider in a nutshell, lapped in silk. Proof against all kinds of devilry."

Shakespeare was not looking at the nutshell. He was more concerned with the weeping, black-edged holes in Stanley's wrist. They looked. as if someone had taken a corkscrew and jabbed it several times through the skin.

"Enough of this talk," Stanley murmured, his

eyes closing. "I grow weary. Tell me of the Company, Will. How fare Lord Strange's men?"

"We continue to be successful, and a credit to your name, my lord. Kit's play *The Jew of Malta* went down well again last month, going some way toward reclaiming his reputation, and we have been asked to perform several comedies before the Queen at Christmas."

"And you, Will? I trust you are writing for the Company now that Kit is no longer able to provide?"

Shakespeare shrugged, knowing that Stanley could not see him. "I am attempting a short comedy about the war in France, my Lord, entitled *Love's Labours Lost*."

"Good. Good." Stanley frowned slightly, His eyes were clouded. now, and his face knotted in confusion. "You know what I require of you, Will? You do understand? We have shared secrets together Will. Remember the School of Night? Remember the oaths we spoke? I pray you, avenge me."

Shakespeare glanced nervously over at the physicians, but they. were too far away to hear Stanley's weak voice. His membership of the School of Night was not something he wished bandied about in the hearing of others. Walter Raleigh's little group of atheists had come in for some unpleasant scrutiny over the past few months. So far Shakespeare had managed to keep his name from William Cecil's notice and he wished to keep it that way. The earl would not normally have spoken of it in the company of other; his illness – or his poisoning – had made him clumsy. Shakespeare could only hope that he had not already said too much.

Stanley suddenly convulsed on the bed, his chest rising and his limbs jerking wildly. Bile and a trickle of dark, tired blood spattered down his chin. Doctor Case rushed to Stanley's side from the window, closely followed by the other physicians. They gathered around Stanley like crows around a carcass, and Shakespeare: found himself pushed back, away from the bed. He was not unhappy at that. Death had been hovering over Stanley for days like a pitiless falcon, and if it chose now to attack he would rather not be in the room when it happened. Quietly. unnoticed, he left.

*   *   *

In the twelve days that Ferdinando Stanley had lain ill, Shakespeare had paced what felt like every inch of the house, the grounds and the nearby forest. He knew the location of every portrait on every wall, every rose bush and hollyhock, every trunk and mossy oak. Ferdinando Stanley had been his friend and patron since Shakespeare had joined Lord Strange's Men at the Shoreditch Theatre as an actor and general dogsbody. Stanley - Lord Strange in those days - had encouraged him to write plays for the company, first in conjunction with Kit Marlowe and then by himself. Shakespeare owed him everything.

And now it was all thrown into chaos by one of the interminable and endless intrigues that bred like lice in the dark recesses of Elizabeth's court.

His footsteps turned, as they had tended to do more and more over the past few days, toward the garden. The weather was warmer than when he first arrived. and there was less of a wind. The trees whispered gently. A flock of seven magpies chattered as they flew overhead to alight on the eaves of the manor house.

The old gardener was busy with a spade, planting a small shrub in the shade of what appeared to be a nettle bush. Shakespeare had often passed the time of day with him in his peregrinations, and so deliberately walked over to the old man.

"I thought you were removing all the weeds from the garden," he called, "and yet you are ignoring the biggest one I have seen since I arrived."

The old man looked up and grinned toothlessly. "The strawberry grows underneath the nettle," he said. indicating the bush, "and wholesome berries thrive and ripen best neighboured by fruit of baser quality. Sometimes there is wisdom in leaving weeds where they be."

"And gentler on your hands, I'll be bound," Shakespeare rejoined.

"That's not something I need worry about any more." The gardener raised his arm, and Shakespeare was struck by the sight of the single leather glove that he was wearing on his left hand. More of a gauntlet than a glove, it covered most of his forearm as well. The material was singed around the top, but it was still a fine piece of apparel.

"Found it on the bonfire," the gardener said with pride. "Fits me perfectly, it does." Seeing Shakespeare's expression, he added defensively, "I didn't steal it, for t'was being thrown away."

"Yes," Shakespeare said quietly, remembering the birds that Ferdinando Stanley had been hunting with the day he was taken ill. "But why burn it?"

"There's some tears in the cloth here, young master," the old man said, eagerly turning the wrist of the glove to display four holes that had been punched through the tough leather. "I reckon that whatever lord found this damage to his fine glove, he decided straight away to buy himself a new one, so he threw this one out."

"But why burn it?" Shakespeare mused. "And why burn just one?" The old man looked so crestfallen that Shakespeare patted him on the shoulder. "Ignore me. You keep the glove. You deserve it, and nobody can deny that."

"You sure nobody will mind?"

"If anyone complains, send them to me," Shakespeare said with some bravado. He was suddenly feeling giddy, as if he had drunk a goblet of warm sack on an empty stomach. Things were beginning to fit together in patterns he had not been expecting. "Thank you, my friend," he said. "You've been more help than you know."

*   *   *

Later, Shakespeare was at a loss to say where he had walked after leaving the gardener. He was so sunk in his thoughts, assembling the: elements of a fantastic plot against the earl in the same way that he would assemble the dramatic elements of a play, that he paid no attention to his surroundings. Eventually, with the characters, their various driving forces and the props they would have needed all assembled in his mind, he found himself at the back of the house.

All he lacked now was a *denouement*.

The stables were busy with farriers and grooms, and he noticed almost automatically that all the horses were present in their pens. There was nobody present in the darkened stone building that housed the various birds - the falcons, the bastardes, the sakers and sacrets, the lanners and the lannerets. They watched him. with glittering eyes as he passed along the row of wooden bars. The smell of bird lime, like *sal ammoniac*, made his nostrils twitch and his eyes water.

The last but one cage was empty. Odd that he remembered all the cages as having been filled seven days before. One bird was missing~ and as all the horses were present it was unlikely that anyone was out hunting. And that meant -

"Master Shakespeare."

He turned faster than decorum would have

allowed, his heart fluttering within the cage of his chest. "My lord."

The burly form of William Stanley stepped forward into the building. The light was behind him, shadowing his face. "I understood you not to hunt."

"Not with birds," Shakespeare said carefully. "But I was wondering what happened to this one." He indicated the empty cage. "The earl's falcon; a fine specimen, as I recall."

William Stanley's voice was calm, but Shakespeare was used to actors and their ways and could hear the tension underlying it. "Alas, the poor creature broke a pinion. We had to have it destroyed."

"Burned perhaps, like Lord Stanley's gauntlet?" Shakespeare ventured without thinking, and then cursed himself beneath his breath.

William Stanley stood watching Shakespeare for a moment, bands clasped behind his back. The meagre light penetrating the slats of the roof illuminated his eyes, making them glitter watchfully. "You are an intelligent man Master Shakespeare," he said eventually. "Your plays are popular in London, I understand. When my brother dies. I shall inherit the title of the Earl of Derby. I am sure that it has crossed your mind that your Company, so well patronized by the present earl, might be at risk. That risk might be… mitigated… if you were amenable to conveying certain messages through the plays the Company puts on - placing what might seem to be unpopular opinions in the mouths of your more heroic characters, or basing your plots around the more neglected areas of our history. Do you understand me?"

Shakespeare gazed into William Stanley's eyes for a moment. "Playwrights are oft accused of ambiguity and excessive wordiness, so let me be absolutely clear. I will not use my plays as vehicles for your abhorrent papist dogma. I serve and love the queen."

William Stanley pursed his lips and nodded. "As I expected. We have had little luck with our approaches this year. I fear. We will have to select those we approach more carefully in future. Might I ask what gave us away?"

Shakespeare shrugged. "Would it make any difference if I enlightened you?"

"It might delay your own demise for a few moments longer."

"A fair point, and one exceptionally well made. In point of fact, the matter that indicated your guilt is the amount of time that your brother is taking to die."

William Stanley frowned. "Explain yourself."

Shakespeare took a deep breath, feeling himself slip into the state of mind he used when on stage at the Shoreditch. This looked if it might be the performance of his life. "If we assume that the earl was poisoned in order to stop his mouth," he began in a deliberately uninflected tone, "and ignoring for the moment the mechanism by which it was delivered, then why choose a poison that takes so long to kill? The answer is obvious

- because the assassins *wanted* it to take that long. Why? Again, the answer is simple once the right question is asked - because they actually wanted the victim to talk. Whatever the victim said must, therefore, be discounted. And what did the victim say? He named his murderers."

William Stanley nodded as if in encouragement. "Go on."

"The earl suggested I consult you over the names of the people he wished to be brought to justice - Richard Hesketh, John Garside and William Houghton. Once I decided they were, in fact, innocent, l had to look around for another murderer. That was when I realised the significance of the glove and the falcon. The earl knew that he was the target of base and foul murderers. and was taking precautions. His food was tasted - by you as well as by his servants - and whilst riding he was always accompanied by armed guards. Another method of introducing this slow-acting poison had to be found. I saw the marks of what looked like claws on the earl's arm earlier, just where a falcon would land when called. I also noticed that a glove with similar holes had been disposed of. That suggested to me the earl's falcon was involved. Its recent disappearance would serve to confirm my supposition. You had to ensure that the claws penetrated the glove - I presume that the leather was somehow weakened to ensure the bird's claws: penetrated – and, as only an earl can fly a falcon, you could be sure that the bird would return to him and *only* to him. But the bird managed a catch before it returned, didn't it? A rabbit that it dropped in the garden."

"It may have done. Why does that concern you?"

Shakespeare remembered back to the moment when he had seen the dead rabbit, its eyes decayed but the blood still fresh on its back. That moment had led inexorably to this like links in a chain. "The rabbit was freshly dead," he explained. "but the body had already begun to decay. When I looked at your brother 1 saw the same process - the dissolution of the flesh while he was still alive, the stench of the grave hanging about him. That speaks to me of foul poison. Once he is dead, I would wager that his body will rot within hours. That seems to be a characteristic of the poison you have used."

Stanley's right hand appeared from behind his back. He was holding a bodkin. Noting Shakespeare's horrified gaze, he smiled slightly. "Yes, and as you have surmised, this blade is coated with the same poison - albeit a much stronger decoction. Obtained from the Spanish ambassador, who would love to see a Catholic heir to the throne of England. With my brother dead and the queen's life imperilled, I will be that heir."

He took a step forward.

Shakespeare couldn't tear his eyes away from the bodkin. "That poison. From the Americas I assume?"

"So I believe. The natives use it on their arrows when they make war on each other.' He shook his head.

"Enough of these pleasantries. Let us bring this to a close." He stepped forward, raising the bodkin. Shakespeare tried to raise a hand to defend himself, tried to move his feet, but his limbs were clumsy and slowed by terror.

Light gleamed on the blade. The last inch was coated with a rust-like brown stain.

The falcons fluttered wildly in their cages.

William Stanley's hand flashed forward, too fast to stop.

The small room was filled with a sound like a muffled bell. Stanley seemed to rise from the floor, his eyes wide and amazed, before he crumpled to the feather-encrusted ground.

The bodkin slipped from his fingers and rolled across the dirt to Shakespeare's feet.

Behind where William Stanley had stood was the old gardener, the light spilling found his body like water. His gnarled fingers clutched his upheld spade.

"I came to ask you if I should put the glove back on that bonfire, like its owner wanted," he said. "Then I heard what his lordship was saying. A damned papist! I never would have credited it if I hadn't heard it with my own ears!"

Shakespeare walked past the gardener to the door of the building and gazed up at the back of Lathom House. His mind worked quickly, shifting logical arguments. Somewhere in the manor house, God willing, the fifth earl was still clinging on to the shreds of his life. If his mind was still intact, and Shakespeare could get to him in time and explain what William Stanley had attempted he could rewrite his will, disinheriting his brother. He could also dictate and sign a letter to William Cecil, the Secretary of State, outlining the papist plot to put William Stanley on the throne. The word of an actor and playwright would not count for much against the son and the brother of an earl. The word of the earl himself would. Dead, William Stanley would be another martyr to the papists. Alive, he could be… persuaded… to list the names of his fellow plotters from here to Kingdom come.

And, if he showed any reluctance, Shakespeare would be perfectly happy to help loosen his tongue.

He turned back and gazed into the building. Feathers fluttered gently in the shafts of sunlight. The falcons all watched - their eyes cold and measuring.

The gardener gazed curiously down at the body. "Is he dead?" he asked, a trace of worry in his voice as if he had only just appreciated what he had done.

"I hope not," Shakespeare said.

"Why's that?"

He smiled. "Because," he said, "there is wisdom in leaving weeds where they be."

A SMALL BAND OF DEDICATED MEN

The backhand blow caught Francis Thompson across his face, knocking him out of his seat. His cheek and his forehead slammed against the floor, sending a wave of sick pain through him. He lay there for a moment, head throbbing and the tiles cool against his cheek, but a hand caught him beneath his shoulder and pulled him upright again. He was thrust back into the wooden chair. It rocked under his weight, almost sending him toppling backwards to the floor again before he could grab hold of the table to steady himself.

"Admit it," the sergeant shouted in his year, "you knew both Mary Nichols and Annie Chapman! You'd lain with them in their filthy whore beds!"

"I didn't know Annie Chapman," he said, tasting blood in his mouth. His lip was split, and stinging. "Mary Nicholls, yes. I'd... I'd been with her on a few occasions, but not Annie Chapman. I never even met her, to my certain knowledge."

The sergeant walked back around to the other side of the table. "You trained as a doctor," he challenged, placing his hands flat on the wood and leaning forward. "But you're a poet now, or so you say. I don't know much about literature, sonny, but I'm pretty sure a poet don't earn as much as a doctor could, no matter how fancy their words are. How is it you can afford any woman – even one as cheap as Mary?" He scowled. "Is that what happened – did you try and take that which she offered but then found you couldn't pay, so you sliced her open to stop her from asking?"

"I… I wasn't eating," Thompson muttered. He couldn't look up from the table to meet the sergeant's scathing gaze. "I managed to scrape together a few pennies from a poem I sold. Mary was very… accommodating."

"Yes, I'm told you were spending all your money on opium down on the Limehouse Causeway. That takes away a manes appetite – and his means to pay to slake it."

"Not all my money," he said quietly. "Not all the time. Just when… when things got too much for me."

"Things?"

"Life."

"Ah." The sergeant pushed himself away from the table, sneering. "The things that the rest of us poor mortals have to deal with. I s'pose those with a more poetic sensibility need something to lean on."

Thompson glanced up at the policeman, feeling a flush of anger over-riding the throbbing in his head. "Yes," he said, "but judging by your nose and cheeks you're more of a gin man I'd say."

This time the blow crashed upwards, smashing his teeth together. He thought he could feel fragments of enamel sharp against the inside of his lips.

"You cut Mary's throat twice, so deep that her head almost fell off when we picked her up, and then sliced her belly nine or ten times. Why'd you do that then? Something you learned at your medical school, was it?"

Thompson felt the bile rise in his throat. He could see, in his mind's eye, the way the wounds would have looked. He'd spent long enough at medical school for that, at least. Mary hadn't been a pretty woman, or indeed a clean one, but he'd lain with her on more than one occasion and she'd been kind to him, even when he couldn't pay her.

The sergeant clenched his fist again, drawing it back for a punch, but the door to the room opened and a constable entered. He drew the sergeant aside. Thompson closed his eyes, savouring the chance to breathe properly for a moment, but he could hear them speak.

"Inspector Abberline says you'd best let 'im go," the constable whispered.

"Why?" the sergeant countered angrily. "What's Abberline know 'bout this cove that we don't?"

" 'E knows you got five blokes locked up in "ere, all for the same murders, an" you're working your way down the line until you get one of 'em to confess. "E says that's not the way things are done."

The sergeant turned to glare at Thompson. "Well you can let him out," he snarled, "because I ain't going to bother myself with it. I'm going to see Abberline about this. How does he expect us to catch this murderer if he ties our hands in the questioning of suspects?"

It took an hour for the right paperwork to be signed, and then Thompson was ejected out onto the Whitechapel streets without any apology. He staggered off towards his lodgings – a room above a stable with gaps in the roof through which rain came in, and a single bed that bowed under his weight so much that he could feel the floor through the thin mattress – avoiding the horse dung and the occasional dead dog or cat left along the sides of the road.

Three men were standing outside the stable as he approached. They were dressed better than most in that area, although their clothes still would not have gained them entrance into any reputable London restaurant. As soon as they saw he was heading for the stable they converged on him, pulling notebooks and pencils from their pockets. Their voices struck his ear in a babble.

"Mr Thompson? Are you indeed Leather Apron, as they say?"

"Why did the police release you from their custody, Mr Thompson?"

"Did you kill Emma Smith and Martha Tabram as well as Marie Nichols and Annie Chapman?"

He pushed his way past them roughly and went through the stable to the stairs at the back which led to his room. They followed him to the foot of the stairs, asking questions all the way and not leaving any time for answers even if he had wanted to give any, but he shut and bolted the door in their face and stumbled up the stairs. Glancing out through the cracked glass of the window he could see them standing in the street, looking up to see if he was still there.

He lay on his bed as the sunlight gradually faded and the pain in his head withdrew. Normal sleep eluded him. He craved a deeper sleep, one that he knew could be found a walk away, in a room lined with rotting timbers and illuminated by flickering candles if only he had the means to pay for it. The trouble was that he was out of cash, and the opium dens of Limehouse didn't extend credit or swap drug-induced visions for medical expertise. Their idea of getting medical attention for a customer in one of their dens was to carry then out and throw them into the street – or into the Thames.

It was dark outside when he heard the sound of wheels on cobbles, the jingling of reins and the snickering of a horse outside. He didn't react – carriages were infrequent where he lived in Spitalfields, but not unknown – but when he could still hear the sounds the horse was making half an hour later he went to the window. It wasn't so much to assuage any curiosity he had: it was more that he wanted a distraction from the gnawing in his insides, and the visions of Mary's ripped body that kept tormenting his mind.

A black two-wheeler was sat outside. The stables were closed, so the carriage's driver wasn't waiting to get a horse shod. He was sitting on top, muffled up in an overcoat and staring down the street. The journalists appeared to have disappeared – probably to the nearest pub.

Eventually Thompson went down to see what the driver wanted.

He looked down from his seat. "Mr Thompson?"

A small bud of unease started to grow in his stomach. "Yes?"

"Mr Francis Thompson?"

"Yes?"

He nodded. "I been told to take you somewhere. I been told to tell you that it's not for the police, an' it's not for the papers. I also been told to tell you that you'll hear somethin' to your advantage at the end of the journey."

"Where are we going?" Thompson asked.

"Brixton," the man said. "I been told to bring you back afterwards."

"After what?"

"I ain't been told that."

Eventually it was curiosity that pushed Thompson into climbing into the two-wheeler.

The journey took them along the Limehouse Causeway to Tower Bridge, then across the Thames and through Southwark. Thompson watched as people, animals and buildings passed by in a series of dream-like and nightmarish fire-lit tableaux.

Eventually they drove up a gravelled driveway towards a small house set into its own grounds. The driver waited as Thompson got out warily. The front door was open, and after a few minutes of waiting he walked through it into a well-appointed hall. No servants were around. That was probably for the good – Thompson's current state placed him even further down the social scale than the servants, and there would have been some awkward moments.

The door to the dining room was open, and there were sounds of movement and voices from inside. He walked across the hall and entered.

The dining table was clear, apart from several decanters, some crystal glasses and a gasogene. Eight men were standing in small groups, looking awkward. Judging by their clothing, they crossed several different classes within London society. Most of them had bruises on their faces, and one or two had torn knuckles.

Thompson stared at the men in the room. They, in turn, stared back at him. Noticing that they all held drinks, Thompson steeled himself and then crossed the room to the table and took a glass. As he was pouring what smelled like brandy from one of the decanters he heard someone in the doorway.

"Gentlemen, we are quorate I believe. Please take your seats."

The man who had entered was tall, finely featured, with black hair that was drawn severely to either side from a central parting. He moved to the head of the table as everyone sat, apart from a massively built and roughly dressed man with a huge moustache which hid his lower face. The big man took a step forward and said, in a thickly accented voice: "What is this? Why are we here?"

The tall newcomer gestured to the last remaining seat. "Please, join us and I will explain."

The moustachioed man hesitated, looked around the group for support, and then reluctantly sat down when he found none.

"My name is Montague Druitt," the newcomer announced, sitting. "I am a barrister, well known in this city, and this is my house. Welcome, one and all." Glancing around the table, he continued: "Unlike many in my profession, who make a virtue out of speaking at length, I will cut to the nub of the matter. We have, all of us here, been accused recently of being the notorious killer known to the press and in the streets as "Leather Apron". Moreover, and more importantly, none of us are Leather Apron. There may be some around this table who are capable of, or who have even committed, crimes of various sorts, both in this country and abroad, but none of you are guilty of recently murdering prostitutes in London. I know this because I have seen your police files and I have made various enquiries of my own over the past weeks."

Like all of the others around the table, Thompson stared at the other faces in surprise. Had any of these men been in adjoining cells to his, earlier in the day, he wondered. Had they been beaten up, as he had been? Their bruises suggested that they had.

"Allow me to make introductions," Druitt said. Looking to the bearded man on his left, he went on: "John Piser; you are I believe a bootmaker from Poland. Your nickname, unfortunately, is "Leather Apron", which certainly hasn't helped your case."

His gaze moved on to the next man: the one with the huge moustache. "Ludwig Schloski; you were born Seweryn Klosowski. Polish, again, but a barber rather than a bootmaker."

The next man was barely in his twenties: a clean-shaven and nervous youth. "Thomas Cutbush: a medical student. You have what can only be described as an ambivalent attitude towards women."

Cutbush blushed, and looked down at the table.

Sitting beside Cutbush was a man with bad skin and staring eyes. "Michael Ostrog," Druitt said. "You also claim to have trained as a doctor, although I have found no evidence to back that up. You are Russian, for certain, and a confidence trickster and thief by repute."

Ostrog started to climb to his feet, but then slumped back as Druitt stared him down.

Next to Ostrog was a thuggish, low-browed fellow who stared at the table and occasionally glanced around, as if he could hear other voices somewhere. "Aaron Kosminsky, a Polish Jew like Mr Piser and Mr Koslowsky, and a barber like Mr Klosowksy. Interesting, how Judaism, Poland and hairdressing keep coming up in connection with these murders."

Thompson himself was sitting at the end of the

table, beside Kosminsky, and it seemed almost like a dream when Druitt turned to look at him and said: "Francis Thompson, a medical student like Mr Cutbush, but with an unhealthy liking for opium which has destroyed your career. You have written some poetry which has been described as "promising", although I find nothing admirable in it."

Druitt's gaze moved on. The man on Thompson"s left was small, rat-featured, with decent clothes and a moustache that extended well beyond the borders of his face. "Francis Tumblety – you were born in Ireland but lived for many years in America. You describe yourself as a "herb doctor", but it is generally accepted that you are, like Mr Ostrog, a confidence trickster."

Tumblety opened his mouth to object, but Druitt turned smoothly to the other side of the table. "Richard Mansfield," he said, cutting Tumblety off and looking at an ordinary-looking man with wire-rimmed glasses on a length of ribbon. "Born in Germany, you have made a career for yourself here in England as an actor." He smiled. "I actually saw you in the dual roles of Doctor Jekyll and Mr Hyde in the sensational drama by Robert Louis Stephenson."

Mansfield nodded, smiling dreamily.

Druitt glanced to his right, to a stocky man who had finished his brandy and was looking at the decanters. "And finally we have Joseph Barnett, a fish porter." He leaned back in his chair. "We have something in common, gentlemen. Mud has been thrown at us, and it will stick. If Leather Apron's true identity is never determined then our names will be indelibly linked with the murders that have already occurred, and with those murders which have yet to occur. We will forever be in the shadow of Leather Apron – our friends will leave us, women will refuse to spend time with us, and people will call after us in the street and throw eggs and human refuse at our doorways. There is, I'm afraid, only one way to stop this from happening. We must catch Leather Apron."

Ostrog and Kosminsky started laughing, while Piser and Klosowsky sniggered. Thompson glanced across at the other medical student – Cutbush? – who looked back and shrugged weakly.

Mansfield, the actor, took his glasses off languidly and started to polish them with a handkerchief. "Accepting everything you say, Mr Druitt, surely the best thing is to wait until the police apprehend the killer. That, after all, is their job."

Druitt was about to answer when Francis Tumblety slapped his hand on the table. "The police?" he said. His voice held an American twang. "They ain't going to do anything. The fact that they've accused all of us, and others, tells us that. They ain't got a clue and they never will!"

"My proposal," Druitt went on, "for what it is worth, is that we form teams and we patrol the area around Whitechapel and Spitalfields every night between, say, midnight and five o'clock. There are ten of us – if we go out in pairs then we can make up five teams. We look for anyone suspicious – anyone who seems to be following a working girl, or who has blood on their clothes without good explanation, or who looks out of place."

Thompson surprised himself by speaking up. "Didn't I read that there are vigilante groups already walking the streets, looking for Leather Apron? Won't we just be duplicating their efforts?"

Druitt nodded. "A fair point, Mr Thompson. A man named George Lusk, a builder and decorator by trade, has set up the Whitechapel Vigilance Committee," mainly because the work of Leather Apron is keeping people out of the East of this city and depriving business of custom. His men patrol the streets at night, yes, but they are innocents abroad. They don't know what they are looking for, and they don't know what to do if they find it. They are more for show and for bluster than for any practical purpose." He looked around the table, meeting every man's eye. "We know those streets better than they do, and we have a much more personal reason to identify Leather Apron. We can succeed where they will undoubtedly fail."

Ostrog stared at Druitt, a sneer on his face. "You know those streets, do you? You, with your fine house and your fine brandy? What do you know of these places, where we live and work."

Druitt looked away, towards the fireplace. "Oh, I

have spent… many hours… in the East End of London, looking for… companionship of the female variety," he said softly. "I knew both Emma Smith and Martha Tabram – not well, but intimately, you might say. I have as much reason as you to want Leather Apron identified, and I believe I have as much knowledge of the locality as you do."

It was the young medical student, Cutbush, who broke the silence that followed by asking: "Why in pairs? Why not individually? We could cover more ground that way."

Barnett, the stocky fish porter on Druitt's right, stood up and walked around the table to the decanters. "I'll refresh myself, if you don't mind, Mr Druitt." As he poured himself another brandy he went on: "The answer is obvious, even if I do say so. We're suspects already. If any one of us is found wandering the streets of Whitechapel after midnight and identified, then the game is up for us. We'll be strung up on a lamp post quicker than you can say "boiled mutton"." He passed the brandy decanter to Kosminsky, who was sitting nearest. "Going in pairs means each man can provide assurance for the other – and nobody yet has suggested that Leather Apron is two men, or three men, or a gang."

"Exactly," Druitt said. He met everyone's gaze. "The Whitechapel Vigilance Committee will fail, because they are motivated by business concerns and by fear. We will succeed because we are motivated by self-preservation, which is the strongest and most basic of drives."

Aaron Kosminsky, who had said nothing up to that point, looked up from the table. "What," he said in a deep and broadly accented voice, "is in it for us? Apart from this self-preservation you value so highly?" He swigged from the brandy decanter, wiped his lips and passed it to Thompson, who immediately passed it on to Tumblety.

"A shilling a night," Druitt said. "Non-negotiable."

"With a bonus for whichever team catches Leather Apron," the actor, Richard Mansfield added softly.

Druitt nodded. "Agreed."

The subsequent discussion went on for an hour, but nothing of substance was exposed that had not already been brought to the table. Eventually, every argument for and against Druitt's proposal having been hunted down and dealt with, they all agreed to join in. Druitt produced a schedule for who would patrol where, and with whom. Maps were brought out and spread across the table with the streets, alleys, public houses and opium dens that should be checked regularly marked. Each team was represented by lines of a different colour, and the lines crossed each other at regular intervals at places where the teams would stop for a while to compare notes. There were also typewritten lists for everyone with the names – well, nicknames such as Saucy Mary and Fruity Tess – of the various whores, hundreds of them in the area, who should also be checked to make sure they were alive and safe. The teams would change composition every night, to keep them fresh, and they would both start and end their patrols at the Prospect of Whitby tavern, where a late dinner would be provided before they started and an early breakfast when they finished.

"Gentlemen," Druitt said eventually, "I believe we have covered all the salient points. There are carriages waiting outside to take you back to the places you live. I shall see you tomorrow night, at one hour to midnight, at the Prospect of Whitby."

The next night, Thompson arrived at the tavern to find everyone else already there, and drinking. He had thought that at least one person would drop out, but obviously the lure of Druitt's money was stronger than the unspoken risks. As they occupied the balcony that ran along the back of the tavern, looking out onto the oily black waters of the Thames, they all boasted of how they would catch Leather Apron, and what they would do to him when they had caught him.

"I hear," Mansfield said, moving up to where Thompson stood, "that a letter was received by a man at the Central News Agency. It is supposed to have come from Leather Apron, although my information is that he signed the letter "Jack the Ripper". The men who run the Agency are debating whether to pass it on to the police or keep it for its publicity value."

" 'Jack the Ripper'?" Thompson repeated. "I really don't think that will replace 'Leather Apron' in the minds of the public. Not at all."

Thompson's first partner was Tumblety, the American herbalist. Their patrol around the darker areas of the city was marked by plenty of fights, some window smashing, various pick-pocketing offences and two suspicious fires, but nothing else. The next night he was with the actor, Mansfield, but again nothing transpired. They saw the competing patrols organised by the Whitechapel Vigilance Committee, but the fact that there were two of them together – four if they were meeting at one of the points where their patrols crossed – seemed to rule them out as suspects. They nodded at the Committee patrols, and moved on. The mood of the city on both nights was strange – scared, yes, but also heightened. People seemed to Thompson to be in search of stronger pleasures, and quicker ones, than previously. It was as if they were poised on the edge of something, waiting for an event to happen but also dreading its occurrence.

He still felt the tidal pull of the opium dens, the ache of need deep in his stomach and the itch of desire in his brain, but he was able to resist – even with Druitt's shillings in his pocket. It was as if the importance of the task at hand had given him a purpose that he had lacked before. Or so he told himself.

During the days, when he wasn't sleeping, he was scribbling furiously, producing poem after poem that stacked up on sheets of paper beside his desk. When he reread them later he discovered that they were darker, more serious than the opium-influenced visions and dreams that he had previously written about. They had an intensity that he had never managed before.

The third night Thompson spent walking the East End of London with Michael Ostrog. Where Tumblety and Mansfield were chatty companions, Ostrog was sullen and uncommunicative. He hardly said three words to Thompson as they patrolled.

At just after one o'clock in the morning, based on the chiming of Big Ben, they both heard whistles and shouts from nearby. Thompson glanced at Ostrog. "I know it's off our route," he said, "but we should check it out."

Ostrog nodded, and together they ran towards the commotion.

A crowd was gathering in Spitalfields, in Berner's Street. A building opposite was lit up, and Thompson could see the painted sign above its door – The International Working Men's Educational Club. Montague Druitt and Aaron Kosminsky were standing at the edge of the agitated crowd. When he saw them, Druitt beckoned them over.

"What's going on?" Thompson asked breathlessly.

"Messrs Cutbush and Mansfield saw a woman being dragged into the yard over there," Druitt said.

His expression was thunderous.

"That"' Old John Dutfield's Yard," Kosminsky muttered.

"When they went to investigate they found the woman with her throat in the process of being cut. The killer ran off. They are in pursuit, and there's a driver of a horse and cart in the yard now who's busy claiming the credit." Druitt made a growling noise in the back of his throat. "Too late! We were too late by moments!"

"At least we can all account for each others' movements," Thompson pointed out. "That's something, surely?"

Druitt nodded. "It is, but I would prefer more. I would prefer us to be able to catch this man in the act, so that we can prove our innocence to the world."

"Who is the girl?" Ostrog asked – more words than he had exchanged with Thompson during the whole of their patrol.

"The word is she was known locally as "Long Liz"." Druitt gazed into Dutfield's Yard. "I wonder," he mused, "if I could get in there to have a look at the body. Seeing Thompson's frown, he added quickly: "In case there is any evidence on the body, or left behind in the yard. The killer did run off in a hurry. This may be the break we need."

"We're not the police," Thompson pointed out. "If there is evidence, then they should examine it, not us."

"You're right, of course." But Druitt still gazed

into the yard for a while, an expression on his face that Thompson had difficulty in reading.

It was near sunrise when they all gathered together again at the Prospect of Whitby. The sky in the East was a watery blue colour, with wisps of cloud, and there were plates of bacon, sausages and oysters provided for breakfast, along with strong beer. Thomas Cutbush and Richard Mansfield were the last back, and they both sank most of a pint of porter each before they could give a coherent report.

"Did you catch him, or even see him?" Druitt demanded.

Mansfield shook his head. "No," he said, "but there's been another death."

Druitt's face was shocked. "Another? On the same night?"

Thomas Cutbush's face was white, and his hands shook as he held the tankard. "We stopped him doing what he wanted," the medical student said. "So he found someone else. You don't want to know what was done to her, you really don't."

"Her face..." Mansfield muttered. "Dear God, her poor face..."

Druitt walked to the balcony and looked out over the waters of the Thames, glittering coldly now in the light of the rising sun. "Tell me," he said quietly. "I need to know every last detail."

By the time Mansfield had finished his tale, Cutbush and the fish porter, Barnett, had been sick into the river, and Thompson wasn't feeling too well himself. The oysters were sitting uneasily in his stomach. Word had come in from new arrivals to the tavern that the dead woman was one Kate Eddowes – a whore, like the others.

They went home despondent. Thompson stood at the door of the stables, one hand on the wood, and thought about wandering off to find one of his favourite haunts: a place where a small man in long robes with a pigtail hanging down his back would heat up a ball of opium resin until it started to smoke, and then allow Thompson to sit and inhale the vapours for hours that would stretch until they seemed like centuries. Twice he pulled his hand from the door, but his feet wouldn't move. Eventually he pushed the door open and went to bed. Maybe, he thought bitterly, the hours of walking and the regular meals were doing him some good.

The next night the ten of them met again. They were all more despondent than they had been on previous nights, and with good reason. They had failed to catch their man.

Thompson was paired with Montague Druitt on that night's patrol. Druitt seemed disturbed: thrashing the black Malacca cane he carried through the air as they walked, as if he was attacking invisible assailants. When he spoke it was in terse snatches. Of all Thompson's partners, he was the one who made Thompson the most nervous.

There was no murder that night – well, not one

that involved a whore and a knife and which couldn't immediately be blamed on a drunken punter or angry pimp. Nor was there a murder the next night, or the night after that. The group still met together every night, driven by Druitt's insistence and his apparently inexhaustible supply of money, but the reason for their gathering seemed more and more remote. This wasn't a calling any more – it was a job.

"This is a success, not a failure!" Druitt cried one morning, as the sun was rising and they were eating their breakfasts on the balcony of the Prospect of Whitby – an area they had effectively annexed as their own.

"Leather Apron is still out there," Barnett observed.

"But he's not killed anyone for a week now," Druitt countered. "He knows we're out there, every night, looking for him. He has gone to ground."

"And, like any wild animal, he will re-emerge from his den when he gets hungry enough." Richard Mansfield removed his glasses and polished them thoughtfully. "Whether that is tomorrow, or next week, or next month, Leather Apron will be back."

"Unless he is dead," Michael Ostrog pointed out. "Or in prison for something else. Or maybe a crewman on a ship, heading for God knows where."

The whole of October went past, and a week of November as well, before Leather Apron struck again. Thompson hadn't habituated an opium den for all of that time, and the miles of walking every night was getting him fitter and fitter. With Druitt's shillings in his pocket he had moved to better accommodation, and his poetry was flowing from his mind like water from a fountain. He had also struck up friendships with the actor, Richard Mansfield, and the medical student, Thomas Cutbush. The three of them had started spending time together outside their regular patrols – taking lunch, and even visiting early shows in the music halls.

It was the night of November 9th, and Thompson was walking with the strange, twitchy Polish barber, Aaron Kosminsky. The streets of Whitechapel and Spitalfields were as familiar to him now as anywhere. He knew each street, each alley, each yard and each tavern. The various whores and doxies would wave to him as he went past, knowing that he was there for their safety. The Whitechapel Vigilance Committee had stopped their patrols after a fortnight, given that they all had jobs to go to, but Druitt's Men went on.

It was that sheer familiarity that almost allowed Leather Apron to escape them. Thompson had seen so many women being escorted into back-alleys by well-dressed men – and intervened many times, to curses and threats – that another one nearly passed him by. It was only when they were on Dorset Street, for the second time that night, that Kosminsky's head twitched, as if he could hear something.

"Screaming," he said. "Woman, screaming."

"I can't hear anything."

Kosminsky glanced at him. "I hear many things that other people cannot. Including woman screaming."

Reluctantly, Thompson followed Kosminsky into an alleyway which ran off Dorset Street and gave access to Miller's Court – a small enclosed space with several doors leading off it. There was a stench of decay and human waste hovering in the air, so thick that it was almost visible. Thompson felt as if they were wading through it to get to the open door on the far side.

"You – stop!" Kosminsky yelled, then cried out as a man in a dark blue coat and a cap pushed violently past him. Kosminsky staggered sideways, and Thompson saw that his sleeve had been slashed through, and blood was seeping into the cloth: black in the moonlight. The man waved a bloodied knife at Thompson, who stepped back rapidly to let him pass. Kosminsky snarled and ran in pursuit despite his injury, shoving Thompson out of the way. Thompson nearly fell backwards into the room from which the man had run. He turned to see if whoever was inside needed help. One look sent a fountain of stomach acid up into the back of his throat.

Illuminated by a fierce fire in the grate, the woman in the tiny and incredibly hot room had been… disassembled. Taken apart. Scooped out. Apart from her arms and legs, which were relatively intact apart from splashed and spurted blood, she had been emptied. Everything that had been inside her was now outside, and her face had been slashed in so many directions and so many times that it was just raw meat. In the flickering firelight the room looked like someone had thrown a bucket of red paint into it from the doorway.

There was nothing he could do for her. Apart from catch the man who had killed her.

He turned and ran after Kosminsky, swallowing the bitter bile that was flooding his mouth.

The chase took them through twisty alleys and empty streets, their footsteps and their ragged breaths echoing from crumbling brick walls. They shouted for help, but their cries were absorbed by the heavy night air. Mist drifted in off the Thames like cobwebs floating in the air. Thompson's heart was hammering in his chest. Kosminsky ran with no grace, bouncing off corners and forcing himself through gaps in walls. Thompson kept catching glimpses of their quarry over Kaminsky's shoulder: the man was quick footed, nimble, and he obviously knew the area well judging by the way he never entered any cul de sacs and found ways around houses – and sometimes through the empty and dilapidated ones – that Thompson had never been aware of.

But they cornered him on a quayside overlooking the Thames. Stairs led down to the creaking wood from the street, but the far end was blocked by a pile of crates and bales. There was no way out.

The man stopped and turned, the knife still in his hand. "Stay back!" he shouted. His voice was accented, just like Kosminsky's, Piser's and Koslowsky's were. Now that Thompson could see him more clearly he realised that the man was wearing a pea coat, like sailors did.

Kosminsky was standing in front of him, blocking his escape. "What is your name?" he asked.

"You're Polish?" Leather Apron asked, wide-eyed. "Like me?" He was barely in his twenties, and fair haired. His eyes were a pale blue. He looked to Thompson as if he only had to shave every other day.

"Nothing like you," Kosminsky said. "Your name?"

"Smaceck," the man replied. "Tomas Smaceck."

"A sailor?"

He nodded, swallowing.

"And the women?" Ostrog pressed. "Why?"

"Because they are diseased!"

"You caught a disease from them?"

Smaceck nodded, embarrassed. "How can I marry my girlfriend now?" he cried. "How can I explain to her that I caught this filthy disease from a syphilitic whore? They deserved it, for what they gave me!"

"You won't have to explain," Kosminsky said. He stepped forward. Smaceck swung at him wildly with the knife, but the Polish barber caught his hand, twisted it, and then hit Smaceck hard on the side of his head. The sailor fell sideways, eyes rolling up in his head thanks to Kosminsky's blow. His foot caught on the wooden edge running along the side of the quay. He fell, gracelessly, splashing into the water.

He never surfaced.

Thompson and Kosminsky stood there for perhaps half an hour, waiting, but there was no sign of him. He had sunk beyond their reach, beyond anybody's reach.

Back at the Prospect of Whitby, and out of earshot of any other customers, Thompson explained haltingly to the others what had occurred. Kosminsky just sat there, staring at his feet and occasionally reacting to some noise that nobody else could hear.

Druitt was surprisingly calm. "We should have brought him to justice," he said, gazing out across the waters of the Thames, "but at least no more bodies will be discovered. If the ten of us are seen around, conducting our daily business, while all the time no more murders occur, then we will stop being suspects. The police will turn their attention to people who died, or went to prison, or shipped out abroad, or had some other reason for stopping the killing. I think that we are safe." He frowned, and glanced at Thompson. "What did you say his name was?"

"Smaceck," Thompson said. "Tomas Smaceck."

"And the girl who died tonight – what was her name?"

This time it was Piser who answered. "The constable I talked with said that she was an Irish girl named…" he thought for a moment, "Mary Kelly."

Druitt thought for a moment, then closed his eyes

in realisation. "Yes," he whispered, "of course!"

"Of course what?" Thompson stared at Druitt, who was shaking his head. He looked at the others on the balcony. "Of course what?"

Richard Mansfield had a newspaper in front of him – an early edition. He was busy scribbling something in the margins of the paper. "The names!" he said, and shook his head. "How could we have known?"

Thompson couldn't see it. "Known what?"

Mansfield turned the newspaper around so that Thompson could see what he had been writing. He had listed all the names of the murdered whores, one above the other, and underlined particular letters in their names.

Emma Elizabeth *S*mith
Martha Tabra*m*
M*a*ry Ann Nichols
Annie *C*hapman
Elizabet*h* Stride
Catherin*e* Eddowes
Mary Jane *K*elly

"He was spelling out his own name, using their names," Mansfield said, amazed. "A pattern that meant something only to him."

Thompson stared at the writing on the newspaper. "And would he have stopped?" he asked, amazed. "Was this it? Would he have finished with Mary Kelly and never killed again?"

Mansfield shrugged. "Who knows? He was obviously badly damaged in the head. Maybe it was the syphilis, maybe something hereditary. We will never find out."

The meeting broke up soon after that. Nobody seemed to want to talk about what had happened, and nobody wanted to go to the police. It was all over, and not in a way that any of them had predicted, or wanted. But as they left the tavern, Montague Druitt got them all to reach into a leather purse that he was carrying. It was their last payment – a guinea this time, rather than a shilling.

Thompson tucked his guinea safely into a pocket and moved to leave, but when he heard Druitt say something behind him, he turned around. Michael Ostrog was standing in front of Druitt, towering over him in fact, and holding up his coin. He seemed to be asking something about it, and Druitt was explaining. Thompson shrugged, and turned to go. It wasn't any of his business.

It was three nights later that the black carriage appeared outside Thompson's new rooms. He heard the whinnying of the horse, and the clinking of the reins, and went to the window to check. *Surely this is all over,* he thought. *We stopped the murders, and we stopped Leather Apron. What else is there?*

Eventually, of course, he put on his coat, walked downstairs, and entered the carriage.

It rumbled and rattled through night streets that seemed, somehow, safer now than they had before. There was still crime and death there, and even evil, but the satanic pall of horror that had been cast over the city was gone. Thompson leaned back in his padded seat and smiled. He had been part of that. He had helped bring things to their end.

The carriage finished its journey around Mile End, rather than at Druitt's house in Brixton. Confused, Thompson got out. The night air was cold, and his breath frosted in front of his face. Ahead of him was a shack built on a patch of waste ground. A donkey grazed incuriously on the scabby grass around the shack.

The door was open. Thompson walked across to it.

The other nine men were inside. They were clustered on one side, all staring across to the other side with unreadable expressions on their faces. Thompson followed their gazes, feeling the questions piling up in his throat unable to get past the lump that was forming there.

A metal-framed bed was pushed up against the wall on the other side of the shack. On the bed was a girl: plump, red-haired, freckled, naked. She had been... spread out. The flesh between her fingers had been carefully sliced through down to the wrists and pulled apart. The flesh between her toes had been sliced through to the ankles and similarly pulled apart.

Her hands and feet looked like splayed red spiders. Her attacker hadn't finished with the extremities however: the ulna and radius of her forearms and the tibia and fibia of her lower legs had also been separated with a sharp knife, and the bones pulled apart until they were almost at right angles. Her chest had been opened up and the ribs spread wide in a starburst. Her jaw had been broken apart at the chin and pulled wide. She looked… barely human.

There was a roaring in Thomson's ears, and a feeling of pins-and-needles in his hands and his feet. His brain felt as if someone had wrapped it in cotton bandages soaked in some anaesthetic chemical.

Montague Druitt stepped forward from where he was standing in the middle of the group. He was holding a leather sack.

"Ostrog's work," he said, smiling. "A creditable first attempt. He used to be a surgeon in Russia – did I mention that? He killed several women there – the first was accidental, during an illegal abortion, but the others were very deliberate. In fact, several of our little group have secrets in our pasts – either things we've done or things we've thought about doing. Mr Piser and Mr Cutbush have made several minor assaults on prostitutes in the past, for instance, while Mr Klosowski has poisoned at least one women that I know of. The others? Well, let's say that insanity runs in several families – including mine." He held the leather bag out towards Thompson. "Please – take one.

Everybody else has." He turned to Ostrog. "Burn this hovel down," he said. "Leave no trace." Turning back to Thompson he confided: "That was Smaceck's biggest mistake. That, and killing to a pattern."

Driven more by habit than anything else, Thompson reached into the bag. He didn't take his eyes off the wreckage that had once been a red-headed, freckled girl. His fingers closed on a coin, and he automatically pulled it out.

It was a guinea, but it had been painted black.

Everyone else was holding a guinea as well, he noticed, but theirs all glittered metallically.

"Ah, it's your turn next," Druitt said gently. He reached out and took Thompson by the arm. "Astonish us."

AFTERWORD

Saving Face

I've been interested for as long as I can remember in the differences between what actually happens and what people *remember* happening, and also in the differences between what various people all remember about the same set of events. Maybe it's because I did courses on quantum theory as part of my physics degree. Maybe it's just the way my own mind works. Regardless, I came up with the idea of aliens who used biological weapons not to overtly attack humanity but to subtly influence it from within. I'd vaguely thought about writing a whole series of stories about these aliens, who I called the Cimliss, but in the end they merely get referenced in a couple of other stories I wrote afterwards before making an actual appearance in 'Dependence Day' (details of which are discussed below). 'Saving Face' was submitted to, and published in, an American SF anthology series called *Full Spectrum* that had been running for a few years. I remember getting a phone call from one of the editorial team telling me that they were going to take the story largely because, at the editorial meetings, the team kept wanting to talk about the idea of living cameras.

No Experience Necessary

This story had been banging around in my mind for a while before I wrote it. More of a mood piece than anything else, it owes something (well, to be honest, probably more than something) to George R. R. Martin's story 'Trucks', in which the romance and wide-eyed wonder of space travel has been replaced by a kind-of bored blue-collar acceptance. I think I also had Stephen King's short fiction from the collection *Night Shift* in my mind as well when I was writing it. Space is just another destination, like Birmingham, and the spacecraft travelling through it still need to be loaded up with cargo. Maybe the feeling dates from the time when I was taking lots of National Express coaches to various places around the country – starting off in one concrete bus station (ah, London Victoria, we meet again) and ending up in another one (hello Portsmouth; hello Coventry), and in between watching the motorway and the rough suburbs of large towns drift by. The story was published in the sadly short-lived UK SF magazine *Odyssey*, edited by my friend Liz Holliday.

Lovers, and Other Strangers

I was so pleased to have been published (once) in *Interzone*, which for a time was pretty much the UK's only professional marketplace for science fiction stories. This particular story is more of a mood piece than anything else, and highlights again my interest in quantum effects (I am still a physicist at heart), ambiguity and unreliable narrators. You can't get much more unreliable than someone whose memories have been influenced by an alien quantum field. Or can you?

Dependence Day

This story was written for *Decalog 4* - a collection of *Doctor Who*-related stories that I edited along with long-time friend Justin Richards. By then Virgin Books had lost the licence to publish their *Doctor Who*-related fiction, but they had built up their own continuity of characters and events, and still wanted to publish books for their established fan base. The central idea for this collection was to take a companion that I had created for the Virgin *Doctor Who* book *Original Sin* – Roz Forrester – and explore the future history of the human race through various stories about her ancestors and her descendants. This was the last story in the collection, and was written with Justin.

Blood on the Tracks / A Fleeting Glimpse

Rebecca Levene, who had been my editor at Virgin Books, asked me to contribute a story to a Big Finish anthology she was editing about another *Doctor Who* companion created for Virgin – this one being Bernice Summerfield, who had first come to life in a story by the immensely talented Paul Cornell. The story I wrote alternated things that were happening to Bernice with things that had previously happened to her father – actually, a different story that I had written a year or so before but never found a market for. The collision between the two stories was never terribly satisfactory, so I've taken the opportunity now of levering them apart. Or, using a word I learned in my Physics degree, *deinterleaving* them. I think – I *hope* – they work better this way. The copyright situation concerning Bernice Summerfield is slightly complicated now, so I've renamed the character as Katie Forrester for this anthology. Out of interest, the idea for the *Blood on the Tracks* segment came to me during the period of several years when I was commuting by train to London. Sometimes the train would stop at signals, and I'd notice fox holes in the bank of earth by the side of the track. I used to wonder what the foxes would do if the train had actually crashed and bodies were strewn along the side of the track. They'd probably eat the bodies, I thought, and then I wondered what the response of the authorities would be. Extermination of the foxes, probably. And thus a story was born.

Only Connect

Another story for a *Doctor Who* anthology of stories, this one edited by Richard Salter. I modified it from an unpublished story I'd written about time travellers coming back to our present and working as taxi drivers to glean those little details about history that get lost along the way. In the published version, the time traveller was the Fourth Doctor; I've reworked the story for this anthology so that the time traveller is as anonymous as he was in the original version.

The Old, Old Story

I sent this to an anthology of horror stories called *The Weerde* that was being edited by Mary Gentle and Roz Kaveney. It was rejected, so I rewrote it for submission to a different anthology – this one being *The Ultimate Dragon*, edited by Keith DeCandido. This time it was accepted. It is, at heart, a werewolf story, but it's about dragons. If that proves anything it's that you can take a story and rewrite in in various directions for various markets if you need to.

Crawling From the Wreckage

This was, for all intents and purposes, the first "proper" story I ever wrote and sold. It was based partly on stories I'd heard about the strange geography of the area around Portland Bay (near, coincidentally, where I now live) and also partly on what some things I was going through in my personal life at the time (thus making it probably the only partly-autobiographical story I've ever written). I sold it to *The Ultimate Witch*, which was a companion anthology to *The Ultimate Dragon*, and also edited by Keith DeCandido. Rereading it now, it worries me how close it is to an old 1970s horror movie called *DOOMWATCH*.

As Near to Flame as Lust to Smoke

One of my occasional forays into writing something with a historical – or at least vaguely historical – basis, this story was put together for a collection of mysteries and crime stories taking their inspiration from the plays of William Shakespeare. *Pericles, Prince of Tyre* is one of the Bard's lesser-known and lesser-regarded works (there are good reasons for that, as I discovered when I saw the play once at the Young Vic Theatre in London). I chose it as my starting point on the basis that everyone else would be going for *Hamlet* or *Romeo and Juliet,* meaning that I would have less competition. Fortunately, it worked…

The Gaze of the Falcon

Edited, like *Shakespearian Mysteries*, by the ubiquitous Mike Ashley, *Historical Mysteries* was a collection of crime stories referencing England's monarchs. Strangely, I found myself putting Shakespeare into the story as the detective. It was shortly before this that I had written the *Doctor Who* novel *The Empire of Glass*, in which Shakespeare also had a significant part. I think I just didn't want to waste the research I'd done. I had vague intentions of incorporating this story into a novel I wanted to write set in the same period, but it never happened. One day…

A Small Band of Dedicated Men

The latest of the stories in this collection, by quite a long chalk, 'A Small Band of Dedicated Men' was written for Maxim Jakubowski's *The Mammoth Book of Jack the Ripper Stories*. Researching Jack the Ripper (for this story, for previous works I'd done and also just out of sheer interest) I'd been struck by the sheer number and variety of theories as to who Jack the Ripper really was. What, I wondered, if all the theories were true… And so my writing looped back 21 years to 'Lovers, and Other Strangers', and the idea that one question can simultaneously have many different answers.

OTHER BOOKS BY ANDREW LANE

Fiction

Secret Protector
Secret Protector
Survival Trials (*awaiting publication*)
War Games (*awaiting publication*)

A.W.O.L.
Agent Without Licence
Last Safe Moment
Last Boy Standing
Last Day on Earth

The 'Six Directions' Sequence
Netherspace (with Nigel Foster)
Originators (with Nigel Foster)

Crusoe
Dawn of Spies
Day of Ice
Night of Terror

Lost Worlds
Lost Worlds
Shadow Creatures

Young Sherlock Holmes
    Death Cloud
    Red Leech
    Black Ice
    Fire Storm
    Snake Bite
    Knife Edge
    Stone Cold
    Night Break

Doctor Who New Adventures
    Lucifer Rising (with Jim Mortimore)
    All—Consuming Fire
    Original Sin

Doctor Who Missing Adventures
    The Empire of Glass

Doctor Who — Eighth Doctor Adventures
    The Banquo Legacy (with Justin Richards)

Torchwood
    Slow Decay

Randall and Hopkirk (Deceased)
    Ghost in the Machine

For further information about Andrew Lane and his work, please head to *slowdecay.co.uk*.

www.ingramcontent.com/pod-product-compliance
Lightning Source LLC
Chambersburg PA
CBHW032221050726
47591CB00001B/209